QUANTUM CAGE

Severn House titles by Davis Bunn

The Rowan Novels

THE ROWAN
NO MAN'S LAND
STAR CIRCLE

Other Novels

PRIME DIRECTIVE
ISLAND OF TIME
FORBIDDEN
THE SEVENTH SPELL

QUANTUM CAGE

Davis Bunn

SEVERN HOUSE

First world edition published in Great Britain and the USA in 2025
by Severn House, an imprint of Canongate Books Ltd,
14 High Street, Edinburgh EH1 1TE.

severnhouse.com

Copyright © Davis Bunn, 2025

Cover and jacket design by Piers Tilbury

All rights reserved including the right of
reproduction in whole or in part in any form.
The right of Davis Bunn to be identified
as the author of this work has been asserted
in accordance with the Copyright,
Designs & Patents Act 1988.

British Library Cataloguing-in-Publication Data
A CIP catalogue record for this title is available from the British Library.

ISBN-13: 978-1-4483-1559-8 (cased)
ISBN-13: 978-1-4483-1560-4 (e-book)

This is a work of fiction. Names, characters, places and incidents
are either the product of the author's imagination or are used fictitiously.
Except where actual historical events and characters are being described
for the storyline of this novel, all situations in this publication are
fictitious and any resemblance to actual persons, living or dead,
business establishments, events or locales is purely coincidental.

No part of this book may be used or reproduced in any manner for the purpose of training artificial intelligence technologies or systems. This work is reserved from text and data mining (Article 4(3) Directive (EU) 2019/790).

All Severn House titles are printed on acid-free paper.

Typeset by Palimpsest Book Production Ltd.,
Falkirk, Stirlingshire, Scotland.
Printed and bound in Great Britain by
TJ Books, Padstow, Cornwall.

The manufacturer's authorised representative in the EU for product
safety is Authorised Rep Compliance Ltd, 71 Lower Baggot Street, Dublin D02
P593 Ireland (arccompliance.com).

Praise for Davis Bunn

"A swift-paced narrative, sympathetic characters . . . will appeal to a wide range of readers"
Booklist on *The Seventh Spell*

"A deep look at how a transition can help heal past personal traumas"
Booklist on *No Man's Land*

"I absolutely loved this story! *The Rowan* is a powerful political thriller that delves both into sci-fi and fantasy. The result is a mesmerizing page turner"
David Lipman, producer of the *Iron Man* and *Shrek* films, on *The Rowan*

"A wild ride"
Kirkus Reviews on *Island of Time*

"A fast-paced, retro-feeling sci-fi mystery. Bunn offers readers a sure guide through his far-future setting . . . A pleasure. This is good fun"
Publishers Weekly on *Prime Directive*

About the author

Davis Bunn's novels have sold in excess of eight million copies in twenty-six languages. He has appeared on numerous national bestseller lists, and his novels have been Main or Featured Selections with every major US bookclub. Recent titles have been named Best Book of the Year by both *Library Journal* and *Suspense Magazine*, as well as earning Top Pick and starred reviews from *RT Reviews*, *Kirkus Reviews*, *Publishers Weekly*, and *Booklist*. Currently Davis serves as Writer-In-Residence at Regent's Park College, Oxford University. He speaks around the world on aspects of creative writing. Davis also publishes under the pseudonym of Thomas Locke.

ONE

Darren Costa wanted to be back he a fraction more than he wanted been running through the same c leaving Cincinnati. There were a hundred and flee. And just one to pull into the bo

He had nowhere else to go.

Cutting the motor carried a hint of defe have been furious. Darren could hear her as well have been seated there beside hir that almost wrecked his life? And for what everything they spent thirty-three years b

Sort of. Yeah. Since so much of it was

He rolled down all four windows. A carried all the fragrances he had once c high on earth. Salt and humidity and sun pizza by the slice. Darren had not been b party. The one that left him chained to spaces down from where he was now par a pair of stained boxers that were definitel from head to toe. Including his hair. The fuchsia he had worn for his wedding. An the first three weeks of married bliss.

The day of their wedding, Gina had ar retired one-star Marine general. The two c a while before his soon-to-be father-in-la about this?'

In reply, Gina settled herself down on Darren crouched, doing his best to shield the morning sun. Four hours and counting Gina ignored the crowd of looky-loos. that to Darren had sounded as cold as a bla him from the future they had planned tog

'This is what is going to happen,' she tol

grow up. But that had nothing on seeing his former best friends after thirty-three years.

Then Barry turned his way and called, 'We're waiting here.'

Which was good for a smile, because he realized they had been aware all along that he'd showed up. After telling Barry there was no way on earth he was driving down. Meeting them at the prescribed time and place. Returning to the scene of the crime.

The three of them watched Darren rise from the car and work out kinks from two and a half days on the road. Barry asked, 'You OK there, sport?'

'It's good to see you guys,' Darren told them.

And strangely enough, it was.

Tanaka checked his watch, announced, 'The launch clock is ticking.'

Barry started down the walk alone. 'Darren, saddle up and follow my ride.'

Barry's vehicle of choice was another sign the world had turned: a new Audi Q8, their top-of-the line luxury SUV. This from a guy who had lived the four months prior to Darren's wedding in a ratty surfer's van parked in Tanaka's backyard, because Barry's folks had grown disgusted over his total lack of drive and kicked him out.

Darren followed him north on A1A, the oceanfront highway running from Jacksonville to Miami. Six miles later, Barry pulled into the lot of an upscale restaurant Darren did not recognize. Barry drove around back and directed him into a slot marked 'Employees Only'. As Darren slipped into the Audi's passenger seat, the kitchen door opened and a woman in crisp chef's whites waved a salute and retreated inside.

Darren asked, 'This is your place?'

'You skip town for thirty-three years, you're bound to miss a few things.' Barry turned north on A1A, then used a red traffic light to inspect him. 'I won't lie. It's a shock seeing you again.'

Which was exactly what Darren had been thinking. He asked, 'Where are we going?'

'Here's a question for you,' Barry fired back. 'How long are you staying? Because if this is a quickie-reunion sort of visit, then hello and goodbye, and the hard questions don't need answering.'

'I don't have anywhere I need to be.' Or anywhere else to go, Darren silently added. 'My company was bought out six months ago. My daughter says I'm always welcome for a long weekend.' A pause, then, 'You know about Gina.'

'Not everything. But enough.' A glance. 'I'm sorry.'

'The buyout will supposedly make me a wealthy man in twelve months. The delay in any of us selling our stock was part of the gig. Until then I've got a pension I can live on, if I'm careful.' Darren saw Barry give a tight nod. 'You knew about the acquisition?'

Barry waited until he stopped at a traffic light to look over. His eyes were hidden by Wayfarers, but the expression was tight enough to create furrows from eyes to hairline. 'You're staying? For real?'

'I could,' Darren replied. And for the first time, he realized, 'I want to.'

'Good. Because we need you. A lot.' Barry turned back to the road. 'So much we hired a detective to check you out.'

'What?'

'Tanaka's kept half an eye on you. He travels to Cincinnati every couple of years, first competing in the national karate circuit and now coaching. When this thing blew up in our faces, he asked me to contact an agency I've used in the past. See if you were actually the guy we needed. And you are. Big-time.'

Darren felt like he was traveling a half-mile or so behind this conversation. 'I don't understand.'

'We knew about your company and the buyout and Gina's passing. What we didn't know was whether your background fitted our current crisis situation.' Barry's smile only tightened the age-lines. 'If we had hired an executive search team and designed our perfect asset, your name would have been top of the list.'

'Barry, I'm hearing the words . . .'

'We're in desperate need of a specific skill set, is the short answer. Neil is the one to really explain what's going on. What you need to know now is this: we're in a situation that basically caught us all by surprise. The upside is beyond huge. But right now, in this very moment, we are desperately in need of a specialist numbers guy with no connection to NASA.' Barry was no longer smiling. 'Everything we learned says you're our guy, if you're willing to hit the ground running.'

Once past the Cocoa Village business sprawl, the highway opened up. Barry goosed the engine and aimed for the Cape.

The space complex actually contained two distinct compounds. The Kennedy Space Center was home to NASA's launch sites, the admin centers, and the Vehicular Assembly Building complex. The Cape Canaveral Space Force Station contained numerous top-secret operations, including buildings dedicated to defense and intelligence satellites.

As they pulled into line with other vehicles entering Canaveral's main gates, Barry asked, 'The purple. How long did it last?'

'Three weeks, give or take.'

'I'm sorry, bro. Really. I've wanted to tell you that for thirty-three years. Painting you purple was the wrong move at the wrong time.'

Darren was actually touched. 'You know, it actually turned out OK. Gina and I stayed friends and we held on to love. Making a clean break with my former life was part of it.'

'Not just you. I've stayed straight since that night. It shocked me sober, losing touch with you.' He started forward. 'Here we go.'

Kennedy's tourist entrance was a large and attractive structure, with flags and polarized glass on the air-conditioned buildings and unarmed guards wearing smiles. The tourist entryway was designed to welcome and warn in equal measure.

Canaveral's employee entrance was functional, stern, efficient. Gate One was modeled after access points to any large military base: armed guards on patrol, constant electronic surveillance, careful inspections of all documents. Visitors were only granted entry when authorized personnel arranged things well in advance. Darren knew all this because he'd come here several times. While still in high school, Neil Worthy began interning at the VAB. Darren had been totally jazzed and fairly awestruck when Neil arranged VIP access to several launches for his old classmate.

As Barry crawled toward the entry point, Darren asked, 'Can you at least give me some idea what we're doing here?'

'Again, short answer. NASA is downsizing and transferring a lot of work to private contractors. Neil and his team have been let go. But Northrup Grumman has offered them jobs.' Another truck, another shift forward. 'That's not the whole story, though.'

'He's not taking the job?'

'Yeah. Sure. Probably. Someday . . .' Barry shrugged. 'Carey wants him to.'

Darren's lack of knowledge about lives that once mattered left him feeling unsettled. 'Carey is his wife?'

'Daughter. Both of Neil's wives got tired of living with a man who was really only married to NASA.'

Then just one truck remained between them and the gate. Two gray transport vans and a putty-colored Chevy idled by the gatehouse entry. A young woman and an older lady, both scientists in lab coats, stood beside a female Air Force colonel. They all grinned as the truck's passenger door opened. Neil stepped down, shook hands, smiled at something the older scientist said, pointed to where Darren and Barry sat. The colonel joined Tanaka and Neil inside the truck's cab. The scientists drove the two vans forward, the guards lifted the gates, and together they entered the Cape.

Barry went on: 'That Christmas before you met Gina, your parents split up, Tanaka's dad died, and I was living in the van parked behind Neil's house. None of us had ten cents to our name. And what happened?'

Darren found it beyond nice, recalling the moment when their lives all changed. 'Two weeks later, we were flying to Nicaragua in some guy's private plane.'

'Surfing our brains out,' Barry said, smiling now.

'Three weeks of total bliss.'

'Because Neil told us he could make it happen. If we all did exactly what he said.' Barry gave that a beat, then added, 'That guy with the plane? He became my partner and financial backer. Passed away last year. I'm selling out. Neil has remained my best pal and adviser throughout.'

Darren had no idea how to respond to everything he had missed except, 'What does all that have to do with the here and now?'

Barry waited until they passed through the gate to reply. 'Neil joined NASA while still working on his doctorate at MIT. His last gig was a project co-financed by DARPA. Ever heard of that?'

'Somewhere.'

'Defense Advanced Research Project Agency. Neil had already figured NASA was going to shrink long before everybody else panicked over the coming change. He went to DARPA and started building a home for himself and his team.'

'I take it that didn't work as planned.'

'For a while it did. Then Neil got sidetracked by this new idea. Which DARPA officially thought was too wild, but unofficially came on board. It's all top secret.'

'I don't understand anything you just said,' Darren replied.

'Doesn't matter, not really.' Barry matched the lead truck's gradual acceleration. 'Sooner or later we all get lost. It's part of what happens when you spend time with Neil.'

Most of Florida's Atlantic coastland was overbuilt, the traffic tight, with massive condos and hotels lining the seafront like a string of concrete teeth. The flash and lure of tourist attractions formed a constant rush of sights and noise.

The two space centers were entirely different.

Beyond the main gates, Darren's train of vehicles entered a great green expanse of nearly nothing.

Combined, Kennedy and Canaveral occupied over sixteen thousand acres of prime coastal real estate. The green expanse was segmented by multiple lakes and one lagoon so vast it required an inland bridge. Their mini-convoy passed stately palms, dense patches of subtropical vegetation, then turned down a ribbon-straight road to nowhere. They drove until a clutch of buildings came into view. The bland military-beige structures were identified only by large white numbers painted on their sides.

A man and a woman in blue maintenance suits stood by the central building's loading bays. The concrete platform held head-high stacks of gear. Darren asked, 'What is all this stuff?'

Barry followed the maintenance chief's guidance and reversed into place. 'Leftovers. The main gear was trucked out day before yesterday.'

Once they were positioned by the loading bays, Tanaka formed them into a conga line as the maintenance people operated a pair of forklifts. The lighter equipment went into the vans, then was stuffed into Barry's Audi until his rearview mirror was blocked and the space between the seats was jammed with cables. Heavier loads, most of which were wrapped in protective plastic, filled the truck. By the time they stopped for a mid-afternoon break of bad coffee and plastic-wrapped pastries, Darren was too weary to speak, much less form a decent question.

Even so, it felt good to be here. Doing this. Part of some action that was filled with, well, *life* worked as good as any word Darren could find just then. Too many of his recent days had felt empty of anything. He had gone through the motions because friends and loved ones were watching.

This was different. A great collection of gear he could not identify had all these people, all these backgrounds and levels of scientific training, working in tandem. They shared an intensity, a determination that filled him with something he had not felt since Gina's final illness.

Purpose.

Around sunset their vehicles were jammed tight. They mashed the portals shut, shared weary grins, and squeezed their way inside. As Barry started the engine, Darren asked, 'We're just going to waltz out of the Space Center with all this gear?'

'What gear?' Barry fell into line between the two vans. 'We're just helping NASA take out the trash.'

'I didn't drive all this way to get thrown into some Air Force brig.'

'That's not happening. I said Neil would have to explain.' That was when his former best friend revealed his grin. The one that took Darren straight back and erased the miles, his weary state, all the years since Barry had last smiled in that merry-jester way. Like he knew the world's best secret, and was just totally loving how he was the guy in the know. 'When Neil lays it out, which he will, prepare to have your mind blown.'

'Tell me now.'

'I'd only mess it up.'

Darren could feel himself getting drawn in, sucked back into the sort of jolly mayhem that had made his early years such a blast. 'I just drove a thousand miles because you said it was urgent I get here today. You owe me.'

Barry's smile grew broader still. Like what he'd been after all along was for Darren to beg. 'DARPA *officially* weren't interested.'

'And unofficially?'

'What Neil has come up with is so totally off-the-charts wild, unofficial is as far as they can go.' Barry pointed at the lead vehicles. 'Everything we just picked up is only the tip of the iceberg. DARPA is totally involved. And NASA. But you can't let on.'

Now Darren was smiling. Just like before. Despite himself and thirty-three years of a total hands-off existence, he knew he was diving headlong into whatever came next. 'Who am I gonna tell?'

When they arrived back at the main gate, the same Air Force colonel was standing beside the guards. With her was an unsmiling Black man in jacket and tie with a NASA ID slung around his neck. Neil stepped down and shook both their hands. A few words, and that was it. They were waved through. Out into the open empty expanse of highway connecting the space ports to the rest of Florida.

They stopped in Port Canaveral's huge cruise-ship parking area and dined at a taco truck. The food truck's specialty was whatever fish the boats caught that day, grilled and served with a relish of chopped avocado, spicy mayo, chutney, mango and a piquant sauce. They ate in weary silence, then loaded up and resumed their conga-line drive into the night.

By the time they crossed the Intracoastal Waterway and headed north on US1, Darren was totally spent. He'd been on the road for two long days, battling interstate traffic and fears he was making a serious mistake, turning a sad and lonely season into a monumental disaster. His daughter certainly thought so.

Just the same, his present mix of exhaustion and unresolved mystery was far better than sitting in the house where Gina was no more, watching the clock crawl forward. At least here time was no longer the relentless enemy, and he its defeated foe. Not to mention the merry jester seated beside him, humming along to a tune Darren didn't recognize, drilling into the Florida night

Darren must have fallen asleep, because the next thing he knew the night was total and Barry's SUV led the convoy. They drove a washboard road turned silver in the moonlight. The sight took him straight back to earlier forays into Florida's heartland, overnight treks to cabins and cookouts and hours spent around the fire. Even people who lived all their lives in Florida's metro areas could be staggered by the state's empty interior. Only Texas raised more cattle, only California more fruit. Hundreds of small country towns stubbornly ignored the coastal area's tangled mess. One good blow, they liked to say, and the state would be theirs again.

The road was made of compressed clay and ground oyster shells. Tight little waves were the result of heavy farm traffic and decades of summer storms. They drove through acres of fragrant crops that Darren thought were blackberries but couldn't be certain. The fields were separated by wire fencing and palms standing sentry-like in the moonlight.

They pulled into a paved forecourt, large enough for produce trucks to maneuver easily. As soon as they entered the circle, industrial-strength lights strung from concrete pillars lit up the compound. A fine old-timey house with a wraparound porch and a dozen or so rockers stood front and center. To one side stretched what once had been a horse barn and corral, transformed now into what looked like studio apartments. To the other and set further back was a massive concrete structure that looked like a warehouse – it had to cover a full acre.

'Be it ever so humble,' Barry said.

'You live here?'

'This far from the ocean? Not a chance. This was my partner's. He left it to me and I kept it as my private bolthole. But all that was before.' He opened his door and pointed out the warehouse's loading bays to the others.

As Darren rose from the vehicle, he heard the thrumming bass notes of industrial generators. Painted high on the warehouse's side was the logo of a fruit company whose product he had grown up eating. It was, Darren realized, a refrigerated packing station. Or rather, it had been at some point in the past. As Tanaka organized the offloading, Barry pulled Darren back, saying, 'You look just about dead on your feet.' He led Darren toward the house. 'Let's get you settled before you fall on your face.'

In truth, Darren was beyond ready to stretch out. The road,

the early start, the poor sleep in roadside motels – and to be perfectly frank, his age – were all taking their toll.

As they climbed on to the broad porch, Darren spotted seven massive satellite dishes dominating the rear yard. The largest was bigger than the house. Beyond that were a pair of phone towers.

Darren turned back to find Barry holding open the screen door, grinning. Barry motioned him forward and said, 'Tomorrow.'

Darren woke to the sound of a ringing phone.

He had been so deep inside the dream it took him what felt like hours to remember where he was, and why. He rose from the four-poster bed and stumbled across the hardwood floor to the chair where he'd dropped his trousers. He fished out his phone, mumbled a hello.

'You promised to call me!'

Trish, his daughter, had all of her mother's precise manner and none of the charm. A difficult marriage and three preteen children had pared away her fragile sense of humor. Darren replied, 'We didn't get here until late.'

'You're back with those awful people! I *knew* it!'

'They're not—'

'I can't believe Grandad said you should go. I can't believe you *went*!'

Twelve years earlier, Darren had thrown out his back. He had taken the lengthy recovery as a warning, and started a morning routine that was part yoga, part Pilates and part core strengthening. Thirty minutes of reminding his body it needed to behave.

Darren put the phone on speaker, set it on the floor, and stretched out on what appeared to be a genuine Persian carpet. He began his routine and let her vent. Arguing with Trish got them nowhere. Sooner or later she would run out of steam, and they could talk. In the meantime, he grunted a response when he figured one was required, and pretty much ignored everything else.

Five minutes later, there was a knock on the door. Darren rose and walked over. He nodded a greeting to Barry, accepted the steaming mug of coffee, motioned for Barry to enter, put a finger to his lips as a signal for silence, then resumed his position.

'Daddy?'

'Still here, darling.'

'How long are you staying?'

'A while yet. They need me to help—'

'Mom would be *furious*!'

Darren set the coffee by the phone, knelt, back straight. He lifted hands over his head and arched high as he could while keeping his rear planted on his heels. 'Actually, your grandad thought she might approve.'

'Really, Daddy? Really?'

'And your uncle. They both said time away from everything might help.'

That silenced her long enough for Darren to swing one leg around and enter an old guy's version of the bridge pose. Trish had always thought the world of her uncle.

Darren took that as the point where a little humor might help. 'Tell me something. Have bikinis gotten smaller? I'm asking because I had trouble spotting the fabric on some of the ladies.'

'They're called thongs, Daddy. As you well know.'

'Did you ever wear one?'

'I'm not telling you that!' Trish wasn't ready to let go of her ire just yet. She persisted, 'I can just hear Momma now. Yelling at you for breaking your word.'

'You know, I think I heard her too. Just before you called. In a dream.'

'And?'

'She sounded happy.' Darren swallowed hard. 'Really pleased I've made the trip.'

She sniffed. 'Probably all the nasty stuff you drank last night.'

'Bad coffee was as far as I got.' Darren could tell her anger was passing now. 'Maybe I should do what you say. Come home. Move into your garage apartment.'

'I've said a dozen times already, you're welcome for a weekend any time you like. Besides, you have a perfectly fine home waiting for you.'

Darren started to tell Trish just how wrong she was. But in the end, he simply replied, 'Give your squad a big hug. I'll call when I know something.'

He cut the connection and told Barry, 'And to think I used to change that kid's diapers. Now she's treating me like I can't zip up my own trousers.'

Barry did not smile. 'Isn't that what having kids is all about?'

'I guess. Does that mean you missed that chapter?'

'Wife number one and I tried. IVF, the whole gambit. Neither of us were interested in adopting. I was too busy building my business when number two entered the picture. By the time I launched into number three, that particular desire had fled.'

Darren shifted to a seated position, grabbed his toes and folded over his legs. 'I actually don't know what to say to that.'

'Some of us just ain't made to win at the marriage game.' Barry watched him rise to his feet. 'Whenever you're ready, we could use a hand.'

They stopped in the large farm-style kitchen long enough for Darren to refill his mug and take the last breakfast burrito from a warming tray. They left by way of the rear door and started toward the concrete structure. The edifice looked even larger in full daylight.

As they passed the satellite garden, Darren discovered his car was parked in a rear lot meant for packing trucks. His Jeep looked like an abandoned orphan. He patted his trouser pockets, realized his keys were missing. 'How did this get here?'

'You sleep until noon, you're bound to miss things.'

Darren checked out the sun's position, realized, 'It's midday.'

'I just told you that.' Barry took them by way of a rear path, past a smaller concrete structure housing the thrumming generators. Darren felt the hair on the nape of his neck rise up straight. A muscle in his back, right where he had almost needed the nightmare surgery, started jerking in a scary little spasm.

'Static discharge,' Barry told him. 'We're working on it.'

As they approached the massive warehouse, the younger of the two lab ladies stepped out. Oversized spectacles were pushed up on top of her head. She was dressed in cutoffs and a T-shirt emblazoned with tour dates of a group called NB Ridaz.

She was, Darren realized, a genuine Latina beauty. He guessed her age at early thirties, but her expression belonged to someone twice her age. Maybe three times. Hard, suspicious, pinched tight. And exhausted.

'Darren, Leila. Dr Leila when she's in a mood.'

The woman, Darren thought, smoked like a man. She pulled a single cigarette from her pocket, flicked the lighter, dragged deep, shoved out words with the smoke. 'So. This is the famous Dr Purple who's just going to jump in and save our commercial bacon?'

Darren looked at Barry.

His pal shrugged. 'I guess Neil wanted to explain why you'd probably refuse to join us.'

'Go ahead, decline the invite.' More smoke. 'Save us the unnecessary grief.'

Barry sighed, stepped around her, pulled open the metal door. As they entered, Leila snapped, 'We're still waiting on that coffee. Like, hours.'

'Coming.' When it clanged shut behind them, he said, 'A regular ray of Latina sunshine, that one.'

When Darren's eyes adjusted, he realized the team had evidently worked through the night. The equipment and cables now formed an orderly circle around what appeared to be a stage covered in rubber decking. On it stood a glass cage. As in, nothing but glass. Even the joints were formed of some polymer. In its center was a clear plastic stool.

Neil stood on a ladder adjusting a conical device so that it aimed at the stool. 'How's that?'

The older female scientist was lost behind a stack of gear. She called back, 'Just a smidgen to the left.'

Neil took a rubber mallet hanging from a beltloop and gave the device a whack.

The woman's head emerged from the electronic cave. 'Your other left.'

'Oh. Sorry.' He switched hands and tapped.

'Once more. OK, that's it.' She disappeared. 'Calibrating.'

Darren counted eleven more identical devices aimed at the stool. The warehouse's vast internal space had been partly turned into a laboratory of sorts and was filled with a bass humming. When the hair on his neck rose again, Darren planted both hands against the small of his back.

The humming stopped with a loud *crack*.

In the silence that followed, Neil offered a soft, 'Poop.'

Which took Darren right back. Poop was about as far into the dirty-word variety as Neil ever went. His father was a pastor, his mother a school principal. Neil never talked much about his upbringing.

The woman said, 'Should I bring Leila inside so she can say she told you so?'

'Double poop.'

'Nix on Leila, then.'

Neil walked over, shook Darren's hand, told Barry, 'Looks like we're going to need those laser scopes after all. Sorry.'

'No sweat,' Barry replied. 'I need to drive back and check on that hotel thing.'

Darren asked, 'Hotel?'

'Oh, didn't you know?' Neil's smile struggled against the weight of exhaustion. 'Barry went and got rich.'

'No yet, but soon,' Barry replied. 'If those legal vultures ever stop arguing over the contract.'

'Five hotels, two restaurants,' Neil said. 'Hilton's buying the lot.'

'You mind waiting until tonight for those laser thingies? I might as well stop by my lawyers, scream at how long this is taking. Not that it will do much good.'

The woman walked over. 'Tonight is fine. I could use a break from Leila.'

'Not me,' Neil said. 'I love her like a sister.'

'Liar.' She offered Darren her hand. 'Hi. I'm Anchali. Did Neil really paint you purple?'

Barry said, 'Anchali is an applied physicist from Thailand. Who happens to be very nice, even if she is overloaded in the brains department.'

'I didn't witness who actually decorated my body parts,' Darren replied. 'Seeing as how I was not in the best shape of my life.'

'He was one step away from the OD corral, our Darren,' Neil said. Then, 'For what it's worth, I'm really sorry.'

'For the bodywork, or telling everybody here?'

'Does it matter?'

'Nice to meet you, Darren.' Anchali stepped away. 'I'm off for a meal and coma-time.'

Darren thought she did not walk so much as dance, a lithe

ballerina in her late forties or early fifties. He asked Neil, 'Mind telling me what's going on here?'

'That's my signal to vamoose,' Barry said, and headed for the rear door.

TWO

'When a material heats up, the energy spreads outward and gradually dissipates. This is part of basic thermodynamics. First penned by two physicists, Claudius and Kelvin, around 1850. OK so far?'

'I guess.'

They stood by a wall of glass that overlooked what probably had once served as the packing company's main office. The lone room stretched the entire length of the warehouse, call it eighty feet. Now the only furniture was a battered filing cabinet, two ancient office chairs, and a metal desk blanketed by files and mounds of paper. Neil went on, 'But we've now identified situations in applied physics where this basic law doesn't fit. High-temperature superconductors, for one. Neutron stars, ditto. And the area I've focused on, superfluid quantum gas. Here, heat flows in waves we now call "second sound". First sound obviously refers to normal sound created by density waves.'

Darren had always enjoyed listening to Neil talk science. He had rarely been able to follow, nor had that mattered. Not really. Just like now, he got a kick out of the man and his childlike enthusiasm, even when utterly exhausted. 'Obviously.'

'Don't make fun of me. It isn't nice.'

This from the guy who helped paint Darren purple. 'Neil, if I'm making fun of anything or anybody, it's my own ignorance.'

'Oh. OK, then. Where was I?'

It was just the two of them now. Leila had come in, snorted her disgust at their inability to harmonize whatever they'd been working on, and stomped away. Barry was off making deals and handling hotel crises. The warehouse was cooled to near freezing by the drumming generators. 'I have no idea.'

'Quantum superfluid,' Neil said. 'Second sound is the hallmark of superfluidity. And these hyperfast waves are identical. Which is totally, utterly incredible. Imagine two tuning forks separated by a thousand miles. You strike one, and they both begin vibrating at exactly the same frequency. Down to a million billionth of a degree. No matter where they are, under what conditions, the vibrational patterns are exactly the same.'

'Whoa.'

Neil grinned. 'My thoughts exactly.'

'So that's what you're doing here? Building tuning forks?'

'Oh no. We're way beyond that. But everything else is going to have to wait until I eat and manage a couple of hours' sleep.' Neil pointed to the paper dominating the office. 'Would you mind taking a look at those files?'

'Sure, I guess. What is it?'

'All I know is, Barry and Colonel Alveraz keep saying those forms are time-critical.' He stared through the glass wall separating the lab from the near-empty office. 'Making this transition to work outside DARPA but funded by them is all tied to what you see in there. Mariana, Colonel Alveraz, is here to keep an eye on everything and report back to DARPA when needed. She insisted we find someone who could be trusted and who was totally outside the internal federal network. And they needed to have a working knowledge of government contracts.'

Darren went back to surveying the lab. The ceiling had to be forty feet high, lined with industrial-strength lighting that cast an almost shadowless glow over the vast chamber. All the equipment was shaped into a pair of semicircles, taking aim at the plexiglass chamber set by the opposite wall. Darren said, 'Barry mentioned something about that yesterday.'

'Tanaka was actually the one who suggested we ask you,' Neil said. 'Mariana needed more than his assurance that you were the right one for the job. So Barry hired a detective agency.'

'I'm still a little weirded out,' Darren said. 'You guys siccing a private investigator on me.'

'It's the only reason we knew about you losing your wife. I'm really sorry about that, but the timing, Darren, I have got to tell you, it works in our favor.' He glanced over, revealing the exhaustion, worry, maybe even fear. 'You know how to give the feds what they need, correct?'

'I've spent years working my way through the bureaucratic tangle. But never for NASA. And that other group, DARPA, I never even heard of them before yesterday.'

'A lot is riding on your being able to translate your experience to what we're doing.' Neil started for the exit. 'It's beyond vital. Call it life or death. You wouldn't be far wrong.'

'Neil, wait. Are we in danger out here?'

Neil reached for the door. 'Depends on who you ask.'

Over the next few days, Darren settled into a routine that had him up before dawn and working until the numbers and forms swam in an ink-stained blur.

All sorts of people stopped by. They mostly stayed outside the glass partition separating his office from the lab. Twice, though, Barry knocked and came in and asked if he needed anything. Very respectful, not concerned when Darren shooed him away. Both times Darren was too involved to remember and ask how things were going with the hotel sale.

The only curious moment over those initial days came from Leila. Three times she entered the door and just stood there, arms crossed, shooting her tight, angry darts over the long room. She surveyed the carpet of paper and files and printouts he was building. She watched him fill two legal pads, then begin fashioning three files of his own.

On day four Darren left to refill his coffee mug and returned to find Leila shifting through his new files. She frowned in concentration and, Darren suspected, genuine confusion. As if Leila was being forced to rethink her dismissal of Dr Purple. The instant she realized he stood in the doorway watching, she stalked away. Not a word between them.

Darren found considerable pleasure in the hours. The work here brought back earlier days, the struggle and sweat and sleepless nights he had endured before he finally grasped how to ask the government for money. Of course, federal forms were not all the same. Not by any measure. Yet they held a similar means of communication. Like all of them were written by committee, then proofed by an accountant with a legal degree. The verbiage would choke an elephant. Just the same, getting angry with federal form-ese defined futility.

The most special part of all this work was being appreciated in a watchful, silent manner. Everyone waiting to see if he could make the grade. But hopeful now. Even perhaps a little expectant.

On the sixth day, just before noon, the Air Force colonel arrived.

She wore a short-sleeve blouse of regulation blue with the leaves of rank on her collar and a skirt several shades darker. She knocked on the open door and announced, 'Neil said he thought it was time we talked.' She surveyed the organized mess now covering almost half the floor and said, 'You've been busy, Mr Costa.'

'Darren.' He rose from the desk. 'Are you hungry?'

She turned sharpish. 'I did not come all this way for a meal.'

Darren had been around military types all his married life. What might have sounded rude to most civvies was, he knew, just their way of speeding the world up to their preferred pace. 'I haven't taken a break since before dawn.' He hefted the thickest of his new files and started out. 'You can check my work while I eat.'

Darren matched her impatient stride across the concrete floor, out into the blistering sunlight. He thought he smelled a coming storm, the rain still in a formative stage. The air felt heavy and damp and full of singular Florida smells. He said, 'Tell me why we're having this conversation.' When she did not reply, Darren continued, 'My guess is you're facing pressure to deliver documentation on some very expensive items that have gone missing from NASA's inventory.'

The colonel's brisk stride faltered slightly. 'And if you're right?'

He did not speak as they had crossed the rear lot and entered the house by way of the kitchen door.

Darren had developed a deep appreciation for the Ecuadorian couple who cared for the house and cooked their meals. There was a placid strength to the pair, a pleasantly agreeable manner that transcended their poor grasp of English. Darren did his best to show how grateful he was. They responded by always having a meal waiting, no matter the hour. Even when he started another day in some predawn hour, he'd find the coffee maker prepped and a plate of cheese and fruit waiting.

Today's early lunch was a frittata cooked to order. Darren took his with a helping of everything they had on offer: rainbow peppers and three cheeses and chorizo and more besides. He accepted their offer of coffee, blisteringly hot and very sweet and tar-black, the way he loved it. Colonel Alveraz was seated to his right, staring straight ahead, not happy with the wait but now willing to give him time. She refused the cook's offer of a plate in fluent Spanish, nodded acceptance to the offer of coffee, and listened as the woman and her husband both spoke at length. Alveraz told him, 'They claim you are a man of honor. I hope they're right.'

Darren slid the file he'd brought over in front of her. 'Take a look at this. If it works, I'll type it into more formal language and have it to you tomorrow. Day after at the latest.'

She left the file closed before her. 'Tell me what you think is happening.'

'There are two crisis points,' Darren replied. 'The federal government by way of NASA is leasing what they claim is eight and a half million dollars of equipment to a dummy corporation Barry set up. And DARPA has leased Barry's farm and the adjoining factory, then offered this same paper company a grant of four million more for NASA to erect the satellite dishes, lay a fiber-optic link to the outside world, and build the four generators and solar farm. None of which appears on any official set of government books. Which brings us to the pressure you're currently facing. Up in Washington, federal accountants are raising the alarm because they can't find any formal record of what this is all for.' Darren pointed to the file before Alveraz. 'I figured the NASA accountants were the more pressing issue.'

Alveraz did not speak once during Darren's meal. He finished the last bite with genuine regret, complimented the cook with a sincerity that had her blushing, and waited.

Alveraz turned the last page, her movements slow, thoughtful. She closed the file and tapped the cover. Once, twice. 'Explain how you knew the procedure for those forms.'

'My father-in-law and his two partners ran an air taxi business. Mostly turboprops, two small Lears. We focused on covering the Midwest states. Didn't try to compete with the big dogs except when it came to pricing.'

'We?'

He nodded. 'I ran the business side of things. Accounting, hiring, timesheets, all the back-office work.'

'Your background is . . .'

'BA in business. I took accounting classes once we moved to Cincinnati. Gained my CPA. That's it.'

She stared thoughtfully at the closed file. 'That doesn't explain what I just read.'

'We began gaining a lot of federal business. My father-in-law was a retired Marine general. His son flew for the Navy, then became our chief pilot.'

'Their name?'

'Gaines.'

She thought, shook her head in dismissal. 'So you competed for the federal buck.'

'Competed and won. After we'd been doing this for a while, a couple of their regional chiefs suggested we apply for leases backed by the federal government. We won seven and added those jets to our fleet.' He indicated the file. 'Every month I had to complete forms pretty much like those, giving precise details to the use and amortization and expenses of their gear.'

'This is good work.' Alveraz rose to her feet, thanked the watchful couple, said, 'Walk me out.'

Midway back to her ride, Darren tried to take back the file. She pulled it away. 'My team can give this the formal polish. You get to work on the next phase. Do I need to tell you what that is?'

'The DARPA files.'

'As far as the outside world is concerned, Neil's team has been cut free. The reality is that DARPA will continue to funnel in the cash required. But everything now is going to be inspected with a microscope. You understand what I'm saying?'

Darren nodded. 'They can't be seen as holding Neil to lax standards if things go sideways.'

'There you go.'

'Can I ask why all this is being kept at arm's length?'

She paused in the process of opening her door. Her inspection was gun-barrel tight. 'You really don't know, do you.'

'Neil's talked about second sound—'

'Not the science. About this.' She waved the hand not holding his file in a wide arc. 'Why they've been shot out here to the middle of Florida wasteland.'

'I've wondered. But to be honest, I've been too busy to press. So has everybody else.' He hesitated, then added, 'It's felt so good doing this work, I've been happy to wait.'

She glanced at the file. 'Enjoying the hours you've put into these pages.'

'Doing a job that needs doing,' Darren replied. 'I figured they'd tell me when the time was right. Which begs the question: is now the right time?'

Alveraz shook her head. 'No, no, you're probably better off not knowing. Find your footing. Do your job. Then go home to your family. Don't plague your nights with worries you can't handle.'

'You'd be amazed at what I can handle.'

But she wasn't budging. 'You can't unlearn this. You can't not worry once you know. Believe me. You're much happier leaving the secrets inside that concrete cave where they belong.'

'I think you're wrong.'

She glanced at her watch, fished in her pocket, handed over a card. 'I'm late. You can call me any time you need help. But not for answers. Understand? That's not part of my remit.'

She slipped inside, slammed her door, started the motor and headed out. Darren remained standing there in the heat long after the dust trail was gone, and the only sound was of distant thunder.

That night Darren dreamed he was on a night flight with Gina, flying first class, something they had always talked about but never done. He was seated by the window; Gina leaned over so far she was almost in his lap. Beyond their window, a full moon cast a lantern glow. Far below, cities flowed past like a string of illuminated pearls.

Gina whispered in his ear, her breath super-heated with momentary delight. 'Isn't this fun?'

He woke up sweat-drenched and his heart racing. In the months since her passing he had been drinking more heavily than at any point since leaving Melbourne Beach. On the worst nights he'd added tabs of Ambien, a mix the doctor had sternly ordered him to avoid at all costs. As Darren stripped and washed his face, he wondered if this was what delirium tremens felt like.

He figured sleep had been defeated for the night, so he dressed and padded downstairs. The kitchen clock read quarter past four, but someone had woken earlier because the coffee pot was full and the brew smelled almost fresh. He poured himself a mug and let himself out the back. The predawn air smelled incredibly fresh, all the dust and day odors washed away by the evening storm. As he passed the satellite garden, something big rustled in the grass to his left. Raccoon, he figured, or maybe a Florida armadillo. Then up ahead he spotted the lovely Leila leaning against the wall by the steel exit, fishing in the pocket of her lab coat for a cigarette. Darren sighed and walked forward.

She said in greeting, 'Mariana told me you're doing good work.'

'Did she? I'm glad.'

'Astonishing was the word she used.' She flicked the lighter, illuminating her strong features. She continued with the smoke. 'I should probably apologize.'

'For what?'

'You know what. How I acted when you first showed up.'

'I didn't notice anything.'

'Liar.' A deep drag. 'But appreciated. I hate apologizing.'

'Can I ask you something?'

'Shoot.'

'Neil gave me chapter one of whatever it is you're doing here. Second sound, he called it.'

'What's your question?'

'Colonel Alveraz said I'd be better off not knowing more.'

Her face pinched in what to Darren looked like genuine anger. 'Mariana told you that?'

'Her exact words.' He watched her angrily jam the cigarette's end against the side of the sand-filled bucket. 'Just the same, I'd like to understand at least a little of what's going on.'

She straightened. Faced him squarely for what Darren thought was the first time ever. 'Good. I'm glad. Mariana was wrong to say what she did. You're part of this now. You need to know.'

'Will you tell me?'

Dark eyes flashed molten in the night. 'Chapter two only. Where this all leads is up to Neil. It's his gig. Agreed?'

'Absolutely.'

She pushed herself off the wall. 'Let's walk.'

'The scientific world is making huge strides in quantum computing at near room temperatures.'

'And that's important because . . .'

'Here's a suggestion. Why don't you try and refrain from the unhelpful questions.'

'Right.'

'Since it would be all too easy to hand you words that mean precisely zip to anyone not trained in theoretical physics. And I'm already struggling to dumb things down and spoon-feed you what might, just might, clarify things a little.'

'Noted.'

They walked the main farm road, the only sound of scrunching footsteps. The coating of ground shells was a throwback to earlier days when oyster farming was a major cash crop and the shells had been discovered to provide a nearly perfect road surface.

'The key here, what makes this so amazing, is how different computers show identical performances. And outcomes. For us, the crucial element is what happens *during* the actual computations. We call this quantum high repetition.' Leila's acidic bite became transformed into the same electric passion as Neil. 'We've been applying this via a construct known as quantum internet. Which is totally different from the one you use to watch adult entertainment.'

'Here's a suggestion,' Darren shot back. 'Why don't *you* try and refrain from the unhelpful comments.'

Her teeth flashed white. 'Noted.'

'Was that a smile?'

'Not a chance.'

'I'm pretty sure that's what I just spotted. A first smile. Maybe ever.'

'I don't smile when teaching kindergarten. May I proceed?'

'Sure. But you're still smiling.'

'You're not helping. Quantum internet is a network of quantum computers and communication devices that take advantage of this repetition. They create, process and transmit quantum states and entanglement . . .' She paused because he had stopped walking.

'The second-sound thing that had Neil dancing in place,' Darren said. 'Harmony. Something.'

The first gray wash of another day showed a face relaxed into lovely lines. 'Harmony works as well as any term. Our language hasn't caught up with what's happening on the outer boundary of physics.'

'That's what has everybody here so intent,' Darren said. 'Devices working in harmony.'

Another flash of teeth. 'Neil said you were smarter than you look.'

'I'm excited and I have no idea why.'

'For once, you and I have landed on the same theoretical page.' Leila steered him around. They passed a shadowy cluster of sentinel palms, bowing their fronds in the direction of the rising sun. 'Quantum entanglement happens when a pair of particles are generated together. The resulting individual quantum states are indefinite until measured. The act of measuring one determines the other's state. Even if they're far, far apart.'

They walked several steps in silence. Darren knew she was waiting to see if he could supply something even marginally smart. Or at least try. He guessed, 'Distance doesn't matter.'

'Good. Very good.'

'Even if, like, they're a galaxy apart?'

'We haven't managed intergalactic travel just yet. But yeah, that's what we're thinking.' Another half-dozen steps. She seemed involved with him now. 'Put three theoretical physicists in a room, they'll argue all day and come up with four answers. I happen to think that in the quantum realm all four answers might be correct, only not at the same point. In what we're doing, time does not enter into the equation. Time is simply not a factor.'

'What about the speed of light?'

She was nodding before he finished shaping the question. 'Correct. Speed of light is the final constant. The unbreakable barrier.' Two steps. Then Leila added, 'In this dimension—'

'Whoa.' He stopped cold. 'You're saying . . .'

She planted a hand into the space between them. 'This is where we enter Neil's realm. He needs to tell you his idea. In his own time.'

Darren knew arguing was futile. 'But Neil's time doesn't enter into the equation.'

A final smile. 'Nice try, sport. Let's go see what they've made for breakfast.'

In the end, they made Darren wait another three days.

No one actually came out and said it. They simply became unavailable for further comments, questions, explanations. Darren minded, but not so much as he might have expected. He had three sets of forms and applications and accounts to keep him busy. There was the NASA-style work he had done first, and then there was DARPA, along with a totally different set of questions regarding specific military applications, stuff he wouldn't dream of answering. But financial records were financial records, regardless of the source. Those he could handle. And did.

The third group was basic IRS-type work, made more complex by the fact that this shell company was not showing profit. Darren worked out what he thought was a fairly solid cost–benefit analysis, keeping the end goal vague, but with a clear attitude in number-speak that someday in a definable future this umbrella corporation would turn a profit. For the moment, he figured he was working just shy of accountant-style fairy tales. But everything fit, all the boxes got ticked, and he went to bed happy with solid hours doing what he considered worthwhile effort.

Which was why he stayed content with the status quo. Darren liked how no one pretended the situation was anything other than what it was. He saw Alveraz arguing with Neil at least once each day. The colonel only went quiet when Leila stomped over and blasted them both, pointing at the work that wasn't getting done and crawling in tight to the officer's face. Each time the colonel did her own stomping, back to the car, pushing up clouds of dirt in her rocket-launch of a departure.

Barry came for brief moments, surveyed the situation, spoke briefly with Neil, not ignoring Darren, not exactly, just offering a solitary wave and then taking off. The man looked beyond exhausted.

Tanaka visited as well, not every day, but close. He had grown into an inscrutable adult with his own aging-surfer style. Long dark hair laced with silver strands, tight caverns emanating from his eyes and mouth. Hands always slightly curved, like his workout routine left him unable to completely straighten his fingers. Darren exchanged waves with him as well. He liked the man's silent way of observing him at work, unmoving and intent, before leaving for whatever it was that occupied his days.

Darren's evenings remained very fine indeed. He worked until he was unable to focus, then retreated to the kitchen and ate whatever splendid fare the couple had prepared. Darren preferred to eat alone, because if he entered when the others were still there the table instantly went silent. He hated being a reason for them not talking about the matters at hand almost as much as he liked how nobody felt a need to fob him off, or pretend things were anything other than what they were.

After dinner, Darren took to settling into a rocker on the west-facing porch. Ceiling fans pushed the air hard enough to ease the heat and keep the insects at bay. The farmhouse's parlor had floor-to-ceiling shelves jammed with books. Most were highly technical texts and illegible as far as he was concerned. But here and there were some real gems. A complete set of Jack London, another of Hemingway. He had selected two books for that night's reading, a collection of short stories by Somerset Maugham and a thousand-page world history that was guaranteed to gentle him into slumber.

He was deep into the mysteries of Maugham's time in Indonesia when a chalk-blue sedan pierced the sunset glow and pulled up in front of the house. Colonel Alveraz. As she climbed the farmhouse's front steps, the colonel shot Darren the military version of stink eye. He offered Alveraz a polite good evening and went back to reading.

Gina's final illness had left Darren living inside glass walls. Even in the center of her tight-knit family, he had remained utterly isolated. Nothing penetrated. In the worst hours, Darren could scarcely make out what was being said when people spoke directly to him.

Being dismissed by their military watchdog bothered him not at all.

When angry voices filtered from the kitchen, Darren decided it was time to sign off. He carried his tomes inside, climbed the stairs to his room, settled into the big horsehair chair dating from a very different era, and kept reading. An hour or so later, he prepared for bed.

When he turned out the light, he glanced out the window. The colonel's four-door was still there.

The next morning he was deep in the convoluted DARPA documentation when Anchali appeared in his doorway. She took his smile as permission to enter and ask, 'How are you holding up?'

'Fine.'

'You really are, aren't you.' She easily made her way across the cluttered floor, a lithe dancer in lab coat and spectacles. 'Fine with us ignoring you like we have.'

'Nobody is ignoring me,' he replied. 'You're just being kept from talking.'

'Leila talked anyway, didn't she? Which astonished our keepers no end, let me tell you.' The lady had a remarkable smile. The expression of a woman wise beyond the hold of time or continents. 'And since it was Leila who talked, our visitors decided it was probably best not to argue.'

'It's nice having these responsibilities dumped in my lap,' Darren said. 'Being able to help out means a lot.'

'Yes, Barry's told us a little about what you've been through. I'm sorry for your loss.' She stepped to the far corner and settled on a rusting lab stool. Two of the rollers rattled as she drew it over. Anchali did not sit so much as perch, ready to take wing if required. 'Everyone needs to belong to something bigger than themselves. It's the only way to know with any certainty that you're not alone on this earth. When life holds that special sort of meaning, even the loneliest of moments take on a comforting note. Solitude simply becomes a part of healing.'

He liked listening to her, the soft music of her words, the caring gleam to her slanted gaze. 'That's exactly how it feels, being here.'

She glanced through the glass wall, out to where Neil and Leila stood by the central plexiglass cage, arms crossed, talking.

'Leila has her own reasons for barriers, and they are hers to share or not. But it was very good that you managed to pry open her door for a walk and a talk. You have utterly astonished the good colonel. Mariana avoids time alone with Leila at all costs.'

'Probably a good thing.'

'How did you feel about what Leila told you?'

Darren liked how she formed that question. Not what he thought. What he *felt*. 'Even the parts that I couldn't follow, I liked hearing. Being truly involved in what you're doing.'

Leila glanced back then. Saw the two of them inside the office and broke off her conversation. Walked over. Stood there in the doorway, arms crossed, watching as Anchali said, 'There is a subset of physicists who believe—'

'Correction,' Leila said. 'Who know. Because we're right. We just haven't proved it yet.'

'That human beings can become entangled. Through love or twin births or perhaps also through experiences. There have recently been a number of experiments that opponents insist were flawed and suspect and nonsensical—'

'They're only insisting so loudly because they're scared,' Leila said. 'Scared and wrong. A terrible, dangerous combination.'

Anchali continued, 'These experiments have sought to show that under certain circumstances, thoughts do not follow the standard restrictions of time or speed.'

'Don't call it standard,' Leila said. 'That's just giving into their Newtonian absurdities.'

If Anchali minded Leila's consistent interruptions, she gave no sign. 'The most consistent measurements show that we experience sensory stimuli in as little as fifty milliseconds, about one twentieth of a second. And under certain circumstances our thoughts actually respond to information even faster, in less than a quarter of a millisecond. Imagine, that means we process incoming data at a speed approaching three hundred thousand miles per hour.'

'Doesn't apply,' Leila scoffed. 'Doesn't matter. Not in relation to what we're doing.'

Darren's gaze was drawn by Neil shifting through the first line of cables and equipment, over to the side wall from which he had a clear view of them. He frowned, crossed his arms, watched, and remained at that safe distance. Worried or frightened or both. But he did not object. Or approach.

Anchali said, 'There are very clear indications, actual experimental data, that suggest—'

'It suggests nothing,' Leila corrected. 'It shows beyond any reasonable doubt.'

'If only,' Anchali said. 'Our opponents' experiments—'

'Designed by skeptics who are desperate to keep their heads buried in the sand! They should be taken back to the main lab and reassembled!'

Anchali's smile carried the patient resolve of a parent allowing their child to misbehave.

Leila took up the telling. 'These *correct* experiments repeatedly demonstrate how certain test subjects under certain circumstances actually achieve an answer to a question *before the problem is stated.*'

The two women waited. Watching him. Darren offered the word he hoped they were looking for. 'Entangled?'

'See?' Leila looked back, found Neil, called, 'I told you he was ready to hear.'

Anchali said, 'Entanglement means one measurement determines the state of the entangled—'

Neil called out, 'Only at the level of quantum tininess!'

'We're talking about a break in dimensional restrictions,' Leila insisted. She yelled at Neil, 'Our experiments clearly demonstrate the same multi-dimensional shift!'

'Perhaps.' He started over, a soft resignation to the word, a fearful admission that clearly left Neil on the verge of anxious exhaustion. 'Perhaps.'

Anchali accepted Neil's worry as genuine. She smiled an apology at Darren and said, 'It's time for lunch.'

'I'll just finish up here and then join you,' Darren said, reading in Anchali's gaze a need to maintain the degree of separation.

She waited until the other two had departed, then turned back long enough to say, 'Leila is definitely correct about one thing: it's time you know everything. Despite the colonel and her concerns.' She started away. 'And we're going to make it so.'

THREE

The next day, Barry entered Darren's office and announced, 'Board meeting in the kitchen.'

Darren had of course noticed the empty lab, and had even allowed himself a shred of hope that they might finally, at long last, be willing to offer a full reveal. 'When?'

'Ten minutes ago. Let's move.'

Darren followed him outside. The morning wind blew strong out of the northwest, gusting to almost forty miles an hour. The palms and satellite dishes shivered and rattled with nervous energy. The air was bone dry, more like Southern California than Florida's Atlantic coast. Darren had taken to checking the weather reports, surf sites and tide charts while his predawn coffee brewed. A major low was developing southeast of Puerto Rico, possibly the first hurricane of the new season. Watching the tropics was another throwback to simpler times.

He entered the kitchen to discover they were all present, the core team. Barry and Neil and Leila and Anchali. Mariana Alveraz was there also. Darren had not spoken with the good colonel since she told him not knowing was the preferable course of action. And Tanaka, who had been mostly absent since Darren's arrival. He knew in that very first moment that he interrupted a quarrel. Leila and Alveraz exchanged angry glares, both women clearly having trouble keeping quiet, even momentarily. Darren paused by the rear door until Tanaka used a foot to push out the last remaining empty chair.

As he seated himself, Leila snapped, 'For the last time, Darren needs to know.'

Alveraz was clearly trying to maintain some semblance of control. 'As I've repeatedly told you, that is absolutely not a good idea.'

'You're not *telling* me *anything*.'

'He doesn't have clearance!'

'So clear him! Have you even started the process?'

'That's not my remit, as you well know.'

Leila sniffed. 'Remind me. What exactly is the role you're supposed to be serving here? It must be ever so highly important.'

Alveraz reddened. 'Darren Costa has been here less than two weeks—'

'As if that was actually the issue here.'

'Your funding depends on following specific protocols. I have carefully laid these out—'

'This is a total waste of time. Maybe you should just go.'

'Excuse me?'

'Darren is part of this team. You're the guest here.'

Alveraz gaped. Rendered speechless.

'Enough of this time-wasting.' Leila rounded on Neil. 'Tell him.'

Darren could not decide whether it was the argument or the topic that made him so excited. Or perhaps it was how everybody else except Neil seemed to be treating this as entertainment. As if the decision had already been made, and this was little more than theater. Whatever the reason, his nerves fizzed with an adrenaline rush.

Neil kept his gaze intently focused on the mug his two hands cradled. 'We're working at the juncture of thermodynamics and quantum entanglement . . .'

He was halted by Alveraz jamming her chair back against the stove. Rising to her feet. Scalding everyone with her glare. Only no one seemed to mind. Neil did not even lift his eyes. He simply waited as Alveraz stomped to the rear door and stood there, smoldering.

Neil continued, 'Our process isolates chained pairs of cubits. Each model has three concerned qualities, or charges, which are actually sums of charges. They govern each site. In our current model, the three local charges are tensor products—'

'Neil.' This time it was Anchali, the older scientist, who interrupted, her voice almost gentle. 'Tell him.'

He sighed. Rocked his mug from side to side. Sighed again.

When Neil remained silent, Anchali began for him. 'It all started with a problem. In a vacuum-like space, radio waves travel at the speed of light. A smidgen under three million miles per second. But let's say we're communicating with a satellite exploring the outer planets. Or we've established a colony on Mars. The distance from, say, the red planet and Earth is between three and twenty-two light-minutes, depending on orbital positions. Which results in huge potential problems for communication. Discussing anything urgent, resolving a sudden crisis situation, is impossible. One single back-and-forth exchange, including interpretative computations, could require over an hour.'

Neil looked up then. Despite the somber cast to his features, the electric spark was back in his gaze.

Anchali smiled and nodded. 'Tell him.'

Neil said, 'Remember what we talked about that first day?'

Darren nodded. 'Second sound. Vibrations in harmony.'

'Right. And?'

He remembered that too. 'Not restricted to light speed.'

'Very good. We think this represents our first real evidence of quantum multi-dimensionality . . .'

Neil stopped when Colonel Alveraz hissed. Glaring at the sunlit glass. Frozen.

Neil watched her as he continued, 'What if we imbedded a message into this shared vibrational pattern. We could theoretically have an instantaneous connection.'

'Not theory,' Leila said. Calmer now. Sharpish, as always. But the rage was gone. 'Not anymore.'

'Over any distance,' Anchali said. 'Distance does not matter. Same as time.'

'This is incredible. Even if it's still just theory . . .'

The colonel hissed.

Darren finally realized. 'You've actually done it?'

Anchali responded with, 'Did you happen to hear about the satellite NASA recently sent to take core samples from the lunar north pole?'

'I don't . . . Maybe.'

Neil said, 'On it was a miniaturized version of our receiver.'

'It worked?'

'Perfectly,' Leila said.

The shared smiles all had a name now. 'This is . . .'

'Top. Top. Secret,' Alveraz said.

'The communication was one way,' said Neil. 'Utilizing this

quantum harmony to send a message requires a warehouse of equipment.'

Anchali said, 'But we know it worked. Proof solid.'

Leila said, 'We sent a command by way of our new technology. It ordered the satellite to radio back an immediate response via NASA's standard comm link. Something that only made sense to us.'

'The answer came back in exactly the time required for the communication to travel *one way*,' Neil said.

Darren looked from one to the next, all the faces now sharing the same electric tension. 'I don't see . . . Why are you here? This should have put you up for the Nobel . . .'

'We were headed that way,' Leila said.

'Sort of, anyway,' Neil said. 'DARPA had already laid claim to our work. Which meant everything was classified top secret. No papers, no Nobel.'

'It would have come out sooner or later.' Leila showed him a tight glint, not quite humor, but close. 'Not even DARPA could keep the lid on this for long.'

Neil looked across the table, sharing her not-quite smile. 'Most likely.'

'Except for one tiny little item,' Leila said.

'Not so tiny,' Anchali offered. 'Not by a long shot.'

'She's got a point,' Neil said.

Leila shrugged. Almost happy now. 'Tiny, huge, world-changing, it happened. That's what's important here.'

Anchali told Darren, 'We accidently established a secondary communication link. Back and forth. Sort of.'

Darren looked from one to the other. 'You just said sending a message was impossible unless the other side had your tons of gear.'

'Right,' Neil said.

'For us,' Leila said.

Darren said, 'Us, as in . . .'

'Humans,' Neil said.

Alveraz did her best to slam the door *twice*. Opening it fully so it whacked the side wall. Slamming it shut on her way out.

Darren waited while she stomped across the rear porch and

down the steps. Car door slammed. Engine roared. Tires spewed gravel and dust.

Silence.

Darren said, 'So . . . aliens.'

Neil said, 'Unless the Russians or Chinese have developed the same construct.'

'Not a chance,' Anchali said. 'They don't have our Neil.'

Darren said it again. 'Aliens.'

Barry spoke for the first time since entering the kitchen. 'Welcome to our world.'

If Leila had surprised them before, taking Darren's side against the absent colonel, what she now said blew away the roof. 'I think he should link.'

Darren took the ensuing silence to inspect the group around the table. Anchali was aghast. Leila smiling at her own audacity. Barry looked horrified. Tanaka was inscrutable as always. All their young lives, Tanaka made a profession of never showing anything. Unless he was stoned or drunk or both. Then he became a total raving lunatic. Which he definitely was not now.

Neil was thoughtful.

Anchali said, 'Leila, please. You can't be serious.'

Leila kept her focus on Neil. 'You see what's happening. Each of us came back with a different perspective. At least we did until we were shut out.'

Anchali protested, 'Darren is not trained.'

Leila sniffed. 'Relative to our experiences, are we? Is anyone?'

Darren watched them. These people who were part of his world now. People he trusted. Even when he didn't understand.

When Anchali did not respond, Neil went back to addressing his empty mug. 'Our unexpected venture resulted in the three of us taking what we now refer to as transits.'

Leila was with him now. Openly addressing Darren. Sharing a hint of her internal zeal. 'You need to understand, going in, everything from this point forward requires words which we don't have.'

'Yet,' Neil told his mug. 'Don't have yet.'

'Right. So Neil went first, then me, then Anchali.'

Darren asked, 'Where did you all go?'

'Excellent question,' Neil said. 'Outstanding.'

Anchali whined, 'Neil . . .' But when he and Leila both looked over, the scientist sighed, shook her head, went silent.

Darren pressed, 'So you've all done this?'

'The three of us, yes.'

Barry said, 'I've volunteered. A dozen times. More.'

Neil snorted.

Leila replied without glancing over. 'How many heart attacks have you had? Three?'

'The first doesn't count.'

'Two are enough to make this definitely not happening,' Leila replied.

'On this one point Leila is correct,' Anchali agreed. 'We can't risk you undergoing the strain.'

Darren asked, 'What strain is that?'

'Re-entry causes a spike in heart rate and blood pressure,' Leila replied.

Darren gave a mental shrug. 'I'd appreciate having a greater sense of clarity going in.'

'Not possible,' Neil said. 'Sorry.'

'Either you go and experience transit for yourself, or you'll never understand,' Leila said.

'We are definitely in agreement again,' Anchali said. To Darren, 'If my opinion counts for anything, you should not risk this.'

'On this one point, your opinion is as valuable as Mariana's,' Leila snapped.

'Leila,' Neil said.

'What?'

'Play nice.'

She huffed, glared at them both, subsided.

Neil lifted his gaze and looked directly at Darren. 'What we're suggesting is you enter the quantum cage—'

'I gave it that name,' Leila said.

'And let us record your experiences.'

'Because we've been shut out,' Leila said. 'Further input requires a new test subject.' She stared across the table at Anchali. 'And further input is absolutely vital.'

The older woman did not respond.

Neil asked, 'So, you'll do this?'

'I guess. Sure.'

'There's at least one positive outcome,' Anchali said. 'This will totally freak out Colonel Alveraz.'

'Maybe that's what the colonel needs,' Leila replied. 'A good freaking.'

Neil offered, 'We've been hoping she'll volunteer to try to transit herself. If it goes well with Darren, maybe she'll opt in.'

'Fifty bucks and any odds you care to name,' Leila said. 'Not a chance.'

Darren could see Anchali still fretted over whatever risk this represented. But she remained silent. Which was probably a good thing, since one small nudge might have been enough to shove him back from the edge.

Finally Neil rose to his feet and said, 'We might as well get started.'

'There is a specific quality to each event,' Anchali was saying. 'Perhaps it is better to call it a unique intensity.'

Leila was hidden behind a curved array of oversized monitors, surrounded by a bank of equipment and cables. Her voice drifted over, almost a shout, 'Try singularity.'

The clear flexible helmet Darren was wearing had fold-down elements for ears and temples. Little metal points poked into Darren's scalp, dozens of reasons to strip off the thing and give his head a good scratch. He was planted on the plexiglass stool inside the glass cage, stationed on a white blob painted on the floor. The plexiglass cubicle was elevated a couple of feet, and below the transparent flooring spread an array of cables and more of those conical thingies that surrounded him on all sides. Like miniature cannons. Minus the gun barrels. He hoped.

Even when disagreeing, Anchali's words carried a musical note. 'A singularity in physics refers to any point where its function takes on infinite value. Such as a black hole, where matter and space-time become infinitely dense.'

Leila shouted louder, her voice echoing around the stone cave. 'Which is precisely what we're achieving. One singularity point resulting in infinite impressions.'

'I must think on that,' Anchali said.

'Think more quietly,' Neil said. 'Some of us are working here. Leila, how goes it?'

'Approaching optimal harmony.'

'Anchali, take your station.' Neil patted Darren's shoulder. 'Ready?'

'My head itches like crazy.'

'Not for long,' Leila called.

'The event itself lasts only a very brief moment,' Neil explained. 'Milliseconds. Tight as a camera's flash. But the experience unfolds afterward. These recollections emerge one after another. Like an unfolding flower—'

Leila said, 'Ninety seconds and counting.'

'Have a good trip.' Neil stepped back.

Leila called, 'Come back to us.'

'See you on the other side.' Neil exited the cage and slid the door shut, sealing him in.

Darren felt as if Neil took the cage's air with him.

Only then did he spot the ER-type alcove.

In the warehouse's far corner, partially blocked from view by coiled wires and packing crates were three hospital-type cloth barriers on metal frames. Only now, from this new position, was he able to see the narrow collapsible ambulance gurney on rollers. Plus monitoring equipment. Defibrillator. Oxygen tanks. Tubes. Masks. IV unit on its metal frame. Narrow fridge and metal cabinet . . .

Neil's voice came through his earpieces. 'OK, Darren, can you hear me?'

'Loud and clear.' He watched as Barry and Tanaka entered the warehouse by way of the rear door, crossed the laboratory and stepped inside the office. Neither man spoke as they took up position. Barry reached out and planted one hand on the glass wall. As connected as possible. Darren waved back.

Neil said, 'Pay attention.'

'I couldn't be paying more attention if I crawled inside your head.'

Leila rewarded him with a barked laugh.

Neil asked, 'Anchali?'

'Recording.'

'Darren, say something so we can test your levels.'

'I tell you what it feels like right at this very moment,' he replied. 'Sitting outside the break, waiting for the next set of big waves.'

Neil straightened from his crouched position, coming into full view. Tanaka rewarded him by lifting both hands overhead. Darren went on: 'The next set arrives, waves big enough to do serious damage, pushing hard as you can to make it over the lip, staring down into that dark maw, the noise ferocious. Every sense becomes razor sharp.'

'Intensely focused,' Neil agreed.

'You're aware of a thousand impressions because you have to be,' Darren said. 'Calm and amped at the same time.'

'Amped and ready to go all in,' Neil said.

'Which I am,' Darren said.

Anchali announced, 'Five seconds. Four, three, two, one . . .'

FOUR

S<small>NAP.</small>

FIVE

Darren felt hands lift him. A *lot* of hands. He was unable to focus his eyes, but he could hear voices, and their words rushed around him. They sounded frantic. But they also did not appear frightened. More like, the situation was critical but not life threatening.

He felt himself settled on a nice soft mattress. The gurney was so narrow his right arm flopped down and he touched cold concrete. Hands lifted his head and fitted a plastic mask around his nose and mouth. A cold breeze pushed in, unpleasant in the sense of holding neither flavor nor smell. A woman's hand settled his arm on the mattress and belted him into place.

Gradually the blurred sounds became recognizable voices speaking real words. He heard Leila ask, 'Any reason we need to freak?'

'No freaking,' Neil said. 'Freaking definitely not allowed.'

'Holding stable,' Anchali said. 'Heart rate very fast. BP off the chart. Both stable, wait, OK, he's dropping out of the red zone.'

'Breathe, Darren,' Neil said. 'In. Out. Stop. Good. Now again.'

'Heart rate down to one-fifteen. BP a tad out of normal range, but moving in the right direction.'

Darren focused in time to see Neil slip off the oxygen mask. 'Ready to sit up? Good. Easy does it.'

Darren felt the multiple hands again, only now he could see Tanaka and Barry standing on the gurney's other side, helping to maneuver him up and settle his feet on the floor.

Neil said, 'Whenever you're ready, try and stand. It helps to walk.'

Leila snorted. 'This from the guy who stayed in the wheelchair for days.'

'Three hours. Less.'

All four of them kept their hands in place as Darren rose on trembly legs. He took a barefoot step on the cold concrete. Another.

Ten more steps, then Neil and Tanaka guided him into a padded chair held in position by Leila. Barry handed him a sports bottle with a straw. He drank ice-cold water, felt the elixir wash through him.

Neil squatted down, the electric spark in his gaze. 'It's important that you speak as quickly as possible. Somehow it anchors the entire process.'

'You pull one thread,' Leila said, 'and the veil blocking your impressions begins to open.'

That actually made sense. He drank again, then nodded.

'Tell us the first thing that comes to mind. Anchali?'

'Rolling.'

He knew exactly what he had to say. The words did not come from a mental process of shaping thoughts. *He described what he saw in that very moment.* The image was as clear as the faces crowding around his chair. 'No one lives on their earth.'

Something about how he spoke, it reshaped Neil's and Leila's expressions. Back behind the first line of equipment, Anchali rose from her station to gape at him over the monitors.

'Their cities float. Each are self-sustaining. Except they're not just cities. They're states. Or kingdoms. Completely separate from each other. Travel between city-states is incredibly difficult, tightly regulated. If one of these kingdoms breaks the code that defines all their existences, that particular city's link to their planet is shattered. They are shot into space. Everyone dies.

'It's been centuries since the last city-state was sentenced to death. But the threat still dominates all life.' Darren shut his eyes. Drank. Focused on what he had left behind. 'It feels like they're not all that much further along the evolutionary scale from us. Far, sure. But not like a totally different level. The cities are placed like this, hanging in air, because they almost destroyed their planet. They experienced a similar ecological crisis to our own. They faced extinction, and this was their answer. The planet is to be left completely off-limits for a long time. Longer than long. Until it fully recovers.'

He felt himself leaking tears. Didn't bother to clear his face. What was the point? 'These sky cities are shaped like triangles. Or ice-cream cones . . .' He felt the surge of power and connection begin to fade. 'I need to rest.'

'Soon.' Neil moved forward, squatted, gripped his arm. 'Focus, Darren. Please. This is vital. *Who is your contact?*'

The strangeness of that word jerked him back. Contact wasn't right. But no word actually fit. 'He's one of four. But these guys, they don't remain isolated as separate individuals. They are apart, then they morph, or flow together, something.'

Leila muttered, 'Are you *believing* this?'

'*Quiet.*' Then, 'Go on, Darren. What else?'

'They're down on the planet, in a hidden valley. It's totally forbidden. They were expelled from their city-state. No. Wrong. They *escaped*. They were already condemned to die for some reason. So they took the forbidden step.' His eyes flashed open. 'That's why they're connecting with me. *They know I'm there.* This bond is forbidden, totally restricted to everyone except a very tight-knit group of people, or conditions, something.'

The images and clarity broke with an almost audible snap. Gone. Like it had never existed.

Neil saw it happen. He breathed, eyes round, mouth open. Then, 'You've done good, Darren. Very, very good.'

He felt it all fading away, the vision and the strength and the ability to remain there in the room. 'How long was I out there?'

Anchali replied, 'We have not yet managed to get a reading on the transit time.'

'Milliseconds,' Neil said. 'No more.'

Anchali said, 'Perhaps it takes no time at all. At least, not in the physical three-dimensional space.'

For some reason, that caused Leila to laugh.

Hands were there to lift and support and settle him back on the gurney.

The last thing he heard was Leila's smug, 'I love being right about how wrong Alveraz is.'

SIX

When he was ready to rise from the gurney, the entire group stayed with Darren, a collective shelter that moved and walked and made sure he stayed upright. The day had somehow shifted to late afternoon while he had been involved in recovery. Darren could have spent hours in the sunlight and shadows and heat. He felt the comforting reality of the here and now in his bones. But his legs were already trembling from the effort of supporting his weight. The others knew it, and only allowed him a moment before gently urging him on. Helping him manage the four rear steps, cross the porch, enter the kitchen, and settle. He watched himself eat from some great distance. Not fully connected, but there.

The only time it all focused was when he realized, 'There's something else.'

Anchali already had her phone on the table by Darren's plate. 'These segmented recollections have been part of the process for all of us.'

'If another image wakes you, whatever the time,' Neil said, 'I'm next door.'

Darren nodded agreement and said, 'The four are a unit. They have been since adulthood or maturity or something like that.'

'Told you,' Leila said.

'Four is the natural size of their . . .'

They were patient with his inability to find the right word. Sort of. Finally Anchali offered, 'Giving us what you can is more important than finding the perfect word.'

'Which probably doesn't exist,' Leila said. 'Yet.'

'Stay with the flow,' Neil agreed.

'This isn't just a marriage like we know it,' Darren said, released from the inability to express fully what unfolded behind his eyes. 'They actually form a single cohesive unit. Only this group of four weren't allowed to . . .'

'Bond,' Leila said. 'Go on.'

'Right. This unification must be approved by the city-state. It's part of their population control.' He stopped, struck hard by what was now revealed.

'Tell us,' Neil said. Gentle. Urgent.

'They were ready to unite. And then the bonding was refused. So they fled. Because at some deeper level they were already uniting. Made whole. They had already taken that forbidden next step.' Once again Darren was halted by an almost audible *snap*. Severing the connection, reducing him to the immediate here and how, was almost painful. 'I really need to sleep.'

'I got this.' Tanaka rose with him.

Darren bade the others good night, and allowed his friend to shepherd him up the stairs, along the hallway, and through the bedtime process. It was like being guided by a human mountain.

Sometime after midnight, Darren's sleep shifted. What happened was unlike anything he had ever dreamed before. Once it was over, even before his eyes opened, he felt as if he had been gifted a new life's dimension.

In that first instant of dream-change, he became aware of the immense burdens he had carried for so long. And yet now, in this incredible moment of easy breaths, he viewed the weight from a safe distance.

He was drawn so far back from his wakened state and all that meant, even time held a different meaning. His awareness was so clear he could marvel while dreaming. How remarkable it felt to question such simple elements from a state of being distant. Being free.

He observed and actually enjoyed the study, watching as time slipped from one point to the next. So inflexible, and yet in this constant motion there was a silent assurance, a soothing constant. How had he never seen this before? A measurement upon which life itself could reside in safety. What a joy it was not to view the past as crowding in, a series of intertwined realities that could never be left behind. Time shifted step by measured step. The past was gone, and the future was an unseen series of infinite branches. Time moved, and the future unfolded as a series of choices made by everyone who lived.

Because of this new perspective, all the burdens he carried

simply became a means of measuring time. Events marched forward, one after the other, held in place by this amazing measure of seconds and minutes and hours and days. Sunrise, day, sunset, night. Time. Passing in drumbeats that never varied. Despite everything.

He observed from this utterly safe distance as time's passage measured out the events that had reshaped him. His wife's illness, the hospital. Even her painful decline, even his fear, all became part of time's travel. He became mildly fascinated, watching how this inexorable flow drew his life and that of his wife's so tightly together, the moments so intense he ached with her, and eventually he died with her. Or at least he wanted to.

Time's drumbeat shifted, drawing him into the steady process of loss and funeral and grief and empty hours. Then the next shift in time's constant flow, and the call from friends who had merely been part of his past until that moment. He heard again the urgent request for him to come back, move against time's seemingly inexorable flow. Return to the area from an earlier time. Resume contact with friends he thought trapped within the segment of time called his personal past. He relived the drive from Cincinnati to Florida's Atlantic coast, and the impossible reunion, and the lab, and the transit, and . . .

Darren woke up.

He lay so still even his breath was restricted. He dared not open his eyes. The dream left him utterly weightless. Darren floated in exquisite bliss, free from all that had drawn him south. He had grown so accustomed to carrying his burdens that Darren had forgotten what it meant to be, well, fine. This was a hard word to apply, when freedom meant life without his beloved. But as he lay and monitored each breath, resigned to the burdens' return, this was how it felt. As if the dream had granted him the impossible distance, away from the existence that had been forced upon him, like it or not.

He was still reveling in this impossible freedom when he fell back asleep.

SEVEN

Darren opened his eyes to a silent dawn. The sun was scarcely above the horizon. He remained a bit unsteady, but able to handle the trek to the bathroom by himself. Beyond his open window, brilliant blades sliced the palms. There was not a breath of wind. He took a quick shower, reveling in how the dreamstate lingered. His memory of events that had come before was still with him. But the distance between himself and everything he carried remained very real indeed.

He began his morning stretches while still captivated by the dream's intense disconnect. He found himself thinking back to other instances when his entire world had become redefined. Leaving his Florida home and marrying Gina. Their daughter's birth. Being made full partner in the family business. Most recently, in his beloved wife's passing. It would be all too easy to view his return to Melbourne Beach as another such transition. But as Darren gripped his toes and sighed down to where his forehead met his knees, he decided otherwise. The previous day's transit, or whatever they wanted to call it, and now this lingering dreamtime, defined yet another monumental change in the making.

Darren dressed and left his room, buoyed by how there was a shred of hope for better tomorrows.

He heard voices in the kitchen, so did not bother knocking on Neil's door. He felt his strength returning, but kept a firm grip on the stair banister just in case. He entered the kitchen to find Neil polishing off a breakfast plate while Leila stood by the sink, cradling a mug in both hands. He greeted them and asked, 'Any chance of a coffee? Breakfast?'

'Coffee, no problem,' Neil replied. 'Breakfast needs to wait.'

Leila pulled a fresh mug from the cabinet. 'You need to anchor the memories. You understand?'

'Give you the first thing that comes to mind,' Darren recalled from yesterday.

'There you go.' Neil slid his own plate to one side and set his phone on the table. 'Recording.'

'They were selected to be culled,' Darren said. As he settled into the chair and accepted the coffee, the group's tragic state flooded in. 'All city-states maintain a rigid number of inhabitants. The culling is simply part of their world. It's not like they didn't measure up. It's a totally random, cold, scary process.' Darren took a first sip. Breathed around the simple pleasure of being safe and facing another good day. 'The wheel spun; they lost. At least, that's the way it should work. But the odds are weighted. There is a secret, clandestine system in place that guarantees the ones in power stay alive. Somehow, these four *knew* they were going down. So they prepped. They were supposed to give themselves up, or die by suicide, something. And they did. Sort of. But it was all a ruse.

'These four know they're going to be caught sooner rather than later. And they've prepped for that as well. In the meantime, they're the first of their race to actually set foot on their planet in a long, *long* time. They're pleased and excited and proud of how they put that together. It was possible mostly because no one has even considered such a move in millennia.

'Everything they see is amazing. Thrilling. Illegal. Communicating with me is part of this.' Darren blinked as the image faded. Instantly he was flooded with a regret that filled his senses with a bitter tint. 'That's it for now. Sorry.'

'Don't apologize,' Leila said. 'This is excellent input.'

Neil nodded. 'Don't worry. The vacuum is temporary.'

'How long does this bond last?'

'A few more hours,' Leila said. The keen edge was there in her lovely features. But the anger was absent. At least for a moment. She was a scientist on the hunt. And he was one of them. 'Fernanda and her husband have gone to the market. And I don't cook. And Neil burns everything. All we have on offer is toast and a plate they left in the fridge.'

'I can make it.'

'Stay where you are.' She sliced two pieces from a fresh sourdough loaf and popped them in the toaster. 'The longest connection so far was about thirty hours.'

'Your input is opening a new dimension to our study,' Neil

said. 'Everything we've gained from our own forays has been aimed at expanding the boundaries of theoretical physics.'

'Partial glimpses,' Leila said. She took a plate of cheese and fruit from the fridge, unwrapped the cellophane cover, and set it on the table. 'Neil, leave that alone. It's for Darren.'

Darren pushed the plate toward his friend. 'I could never eat all that.'

'Our contacts were not welcoming,' Neil said, taking a slice of apple and some crumbly cheese. 'To say the least.'

'They hated our being there,' Leila said, placing the toast and a ceramic crock of butter in front of Darren. 'It made them furious.'

'And then they cut us out,' Neil said. He asked Leila, 'Could you give us a minute?'

Leila offered her boss a knowing smirk, leaving Darren fairly certain the two of them had been discussing whatever came next before his arrival. 'No problem.'

When she slipped out the rear door, Neil said, 'I've waited thirty years to say I'm sorry.' The words poured out in a rush. 'I was jealous. Furious with you. We'd spent years going in one direction. The solitary brethren was how I thought of us. The wild ones. Then there you go, finding what I was pretty sure I'd never have. A woman was taking our place. She threatened us. She threatened *me*.'

On one level, Darren heard his oldest friend. But gradually his ability to pay full attention was pulled away by the onset of another image. Fragile, yet utterly clear. Pressing at him with a need to release.

Neil continued, 'I don't know who actually said the words let's paint him purple. But I know *why*. We wanted to destroy your new status quo. Bring you back. It was the most selfish, destructive act of my entire life. I knew it then, I guess. But I only *saw* it when you weren't there any longer.'

'Neil.' Darren had no choice but to halt him. 'I couldn't have had the relationship I built with Gina without cutting ties. You did us a favor. Gina and I. Really.'

He felt like there were a dozen different ways he could have said it better. A hundred. Then Neil asked, 'So, we're OK?'

'Better than that,' Darren replied. 'It's behind us. Totally. And right now I need to talk about the transit.'

Neil set his phone back between them, hit the recording key, and finally met Darren's gaze. 'Ready when you are.'

Once again Darren bonded with the *others*, the connection forged through this sense of tragic resonance. 'They've been outcasts all their lives. I don't know exactly what that means—'

'Ignore your questions,' Neil said. 'Don't worry about what's not there. It only creates interference and fractures your vision. Talk about what is.'

His *vision*. Hearing those words resonated at the level of impossible contact. *Talk about what is*. 'These four, they suspected all along the culling wasn't fair, and they were doomed. So they went looking for answers. Which was also illegal. And they uncovered proof, real, hard evidence, that the system is rigged. So they decided to rebel. Something about this decision created a complete and utter split between them and their city-state. It was as grave an act as their descending to the planet. Utterly unheard of. They shaped this new phase of their life around the simple concept that they would escape and survive for as long as possible. And the key question they asked themselves was what do we want to do with the days we have left?'

'Like a bucket list.'

'That's it exactly.'

Neil softly tapped two fingers on the table, frowning intently. No room now for anything but the new data.

Darren went on: 'Connecting with me is part of this rebellion. Their linking together is the same.'

'Can you tell me anything about this linking?'

Darren shut his eyes. 'What they've done, forming this unit of four without permission, is totally forbidden. Worse than illegal. It breaks a sacred bond.' Somehow Neil's comments sharpened his focus. Left Darren wondering if this was part of their *own* bonding process. 'These are bedrock commandments that form the foundation of their lives. You must not. Ever. Do. This.'

'But they did.'

'Right. They broke the code, and now their city-state's link to the planet – it's existence – is under threat. And to make it worse, they included me in the process. They're down on the planet's surface. Bonding with me. And with each other. Flowing into a single four-person unit, re-emerging, doing it again. Over and over. They *wanted* me to experience this. With them.'

'How did it make you feel?'

'High as a kite.' He smiled at the intensity of reliving that moment. Then it was over. Fading fast as a dawn dream. Gone in the space of one breath. 'Oh, man.'

'Don't try and hold on. We'll just wait and see if it comes back.'

Darren was filled with a sudden desire to describe the previous night's dreams. But something held him back. A distinct barrier, strong as a spoken warning. So he merely asked, 'Can I go again? Do another transit?'

'Let's give it a day for you to fully recover. Once you feel totally rested up and ready, absolutely.'

'Thanks. That means a lot.'

Neil rose from the table, serious now. Grave. 'Right now, you are our only connecting point to everything we don't know. The transit system was totally closed down until you showed up.'

EIGHT

Darren crossed the rear yard at a slow pace, luxuriating in the feel of light and heat on his skin. He entered the warehouse and passed behind the equipment's outer rim, heading for the side wall where Anchali and Leila worked on poster-size sheets of thick paper taped to the concrete. They drew graphs, discussed calculations, wrote the script of science. Darren smelled coffee and started to ask for a mug when another image rose behind his eyes. 'I may have more input from the transit.'

'There is no may,' Leila replied, her focus tight on the calculations. 'Only do.'

Anchali looked askance at the younger woman. 'Was that a joke?'

'Certainly not.'

Neil checked that his phone was recording, held it out, said, 'Go ahead.'

'They've been hoping to forge this link for a while. It was a determined effort, making themselves open and ready. Joining with me was one part of their stepping away from the code that dictates so much of life in the city-state. One by one, these unbreakable laws are being shattered. I'm a key part of their defiance. The city-state is trying to hunt them down. So here they are. Hiding on the planet's surface. Merging together, four becoming one, and seeking to bring me into this mix.'

Neil asked, 'Is there anything you can tell me about how you were brought in?'

A tight flash, no longer than a single breath. Darren replied, 'One of this group was a scientist. *Is* one. This is how they discovered about the cull – the scientist had access to research and city-state records through the group they worked for. Or with. Knowledge of the culls is restricted. There are also scientists in the city-state who officially have the right to forge this transit link. I think they were your contacts.' Darren felt the bond begin to fade, ending with a final fading image. He added, 'They are aiming upward.'

Leila murmured, 'Of course.'

Neil shushed her. 'Go on. Explain what that means, upward.'

'For those in the city-state, these transit connections with your team are an unwanted by-product of something much bigger. They're intent on connecting to a group or planet or race that is super-advanced. Having us show up is nothing more than interference, like static interrupting a radio signal.'

Anchali said, 'That explains so much.'

Neil hissed for silence, then, 'Anything else?'

'What you did, bond with the city-state's top scientists, happened because they are opening themselves to the same kind of bond. Only their aim is to connect with a much more advanced civilization. Your transits were an unwanted by-product. What happened with me is totally different. This four *wanted* to connect. They stole the necessary equipment and worked to make it happen.' Darren breathed. Waited. Finally accepted, 'It's gone.'

Barry arrived the next day, driving a transit van with his hotel logo on the side. He and Darren and Anchali unloaded a dozen classroom-size whiteboards and three easels intended to hold the graph papers taped to the side wall. Neil and Leila stripped the plastic covers off four whiteboards and lined them along the side wall. Barry then presented Darren with two more bulky files bearing DARPA seals. 'They claim it's urgent.'

He accepted the files and asked, 'Who are they?'

Barry shrugged. 'I'm playing messenger because Alveraz asked nice. Anything more you'll need to get from Neil. Personally, I've learned not to press.'

Darren deposited the new workload on his desk, then followed his friend outside. He thought Barry looked exhausted. There was no hint of the merry jester, no spark to Barry's gaze. 'You holding up OK?'

'Only way I'm managing is by thinking maybe tomorrow it will all be over.' Barry halted by the Audi driver's door. The wind was back in its most common summer form, a steady salt-laden push off the Atlantic. Humid and hot. Clouds bunched and pushed inland. Thunder rumbled a distant note, promising heavy rain. Life in Florida's off season. 'I'm worried about you taking another trip to never-never land.'

Darren started to describe the tight adrenaline thrill contained in the prospect of another interstellar transit. But he couldn't find the words.

When he remained silent, Barry pressed, 'You're determined to transit again?'

'Every chance I get. Everybody else has been shut out. But I'm hooked up with a group that actually wants me there.' Darren hesitated, then added, 'It means the world, having a role to play here. Do work with real meaning.'

'I also heard them shouting about a heart close to exploding.' Barry slipped behind the wheel. 'We didn't bring you back just to lose you again.'

'I've learned to respect my body's needs,' Darren replied. 'Comes with living to a ripe old age.'

He stood in the sweltering heat until the dust from Barry's departure had settled. The palms' lengthening shadows cut sharp edges into the gray-white surface. Somewhere close by a cardinal chimed the hour as he started back.

The afternoon held a unique flavor as Darren settled into his routine. He glanced up from time to time, watching the trio work their way through calculations and graphs and dense scribbles that filled three whiteboards. What he had told Barry was a mere fragment of the truth. It felt beyond great to fill life's empty spaces with real purpose.

As Darren perused the new documents, a clearer sense of their unseen backers' strategy began to unfold. From what he had on paper, DARPA showed no official awareness of these interstellar transits. All these new questions, the forward-looking demands for detail, were focused upon second sound.

Midway through the first folder, Darren broke for a late lunch. Today's feast was flour tortillas filled with spicy stewed beef, beans, avocado, shredded lettuce, cheese, the works. Darren thanked their chef in his terrible Spanish, and when he heard voices coming their way he slipped down the central corridor and out the front door. His internal dialogue made for all the company he needed.

Darren stopped in the shade of a live oak, finished his meal and studied the silent house. Their transits had brought back a glimpse of something even bigger. What that was exactly, he probably wouldn't understand. Nor did he need to. Far more was at stake than him supplying new data through more of his own transits.

Their location in the Florida hinterlands made perfect sense now. Neil's DARPA-funded, top-secret work on this communication project had huge potential, enough to hide them away. So here they were, in a makeshift laboratory sealed inside a disused packing shed, with Colonel Alveraz as their solitary go-between.

As Darren started back toward the lab and his office, Barry's concerns echoed through the hot Florida afternoon. Darren's response was the same, only different. The question wasn't whether he was making another transit. The real issue was how he could possibly help them achieve the interstellar impossibility. Help bring clarity to the unexpected mysteries that the secret second communication link had opened up. Whatever they might be.

Hours later, when Darren finally called it quits for the night, he entered an empty kitchen. He took his plate from the warming oven and ate standing by the sink. He could hear the murmur of voices emanating from the front porch, but felt no desire to join them. He washed his glass and plate and utensils, set them in the drying rack, and headed up the stairs. Darren could feel the weight of fatigue growing with each step. Balancing that was a real sense of a very productive day. He was doing good work. He was needed. As he prepared for bed, Darren felt sated by simple pleasures he feared had been lost and gone for good.

It seemed as though he slipped into this newly redefined dreamstate almost immediately after falling asleep.

The relief of having it return a second time was exquisite. Though he slept, he remained aware enough to be filled with joy, bliss, excitement. All the words worked and none of them really fit. He was asleep, aware, free. The only element holding any force, any importance, was the *now*.

This second experience was similar to the first, and yet quite different. His perspective held to the same utter disconnect, as if his life was, well, purified.

In this second dreamstate, his focus turned outward. He found it a strange word to apply, since he was zonked out and motionless. But it was true. His clarified awareness drifted about, inspecting things with a curiosity so intense he was filled with the pleasure of seeing his world anew. He saw; he studied; he fashioned definitions.

Burdens.

The word had never held such impact. Just as with the first dreamstate, he viewed his surroundings without the tainted coloring that came from everything he had recently experienced. The freedom it carried was almost frightening. Not for what this moment held. Rather, what he would confront upon awakening.

He shifted from scene to scene, or one viewpoint to the next, with fluid ease. The bedroom, the lab, the garden of satellite dishes, the farmhouse, the surrounding night.

Wind.

He returned to his bed and came partially awake. Enough for his senses to be utterly filled by the gentle breeze sighing through the open window. He wondered if he was merely dreaming the experience, then decided he didn't care. The breeze was turned musical by the screen, a soothing hush that carried night flavors of earth and blooming plants and perhaps a hint of the sea.

He woke fully then, and lay as the first time, wishing in helpless fashion for the chance to reside permanently in that dreamstate's newly defined freedom. For him to maintain this ability to be overwhelmed by the exquisite nature of seeing the world anew. Life flooded him with a joy so intense he might have wept. Then it was over, fading away, the moment both tender and intense. As if the experience itself was bidding him a fond farewell.

He remained there, trapped by the loss, for what felt like hours. Until the boring regularity of normal sleep captured him once more.

NINE

The next morning, Darren woke to find everything back in place, burdens as they had been, time just another part of the background. But yet again the aftereffects of this latest dreamstate stayed with him. The aroma of momentary freedom lingered, like the flavor of a wonderful meal.

Darren performed his morning stretches, then showered and dressed. Fernanda was alone in the kitchen when he arrived. Darren accepted her offer of Spanish omelet and biscuits, and sat staring at the sunlit screen door, filled with a simple gladness for being here. He was fully involved now. The transit and these dreamstates had reshaped his life in a way he could never have expected. Here in this converted farm in the middle of Florida's nowhere land, he had found the promise of new beginnings.

He was just finishing breakfast when a battered Toyota Land Cruiser pulled into the rear lot. Tanaka and Colonel Alveraz rose and started toward the lab. Alveraz was dressed in civvies – a sleeveless sweatshirt, track pants that ended mid-shin, Nikes, wraparound shades and a USAF sweatband. She remained an ultra-tight and focused officer even when out of uniform.

Darren waited until they entered the warehouse and the metal door closed behind them. Then he rose and thanked Fernanda and headed out.

When he entered the laboratory, Alveraz was seated at Leila's station with Leila on one side and Anchali the other. Tanaka and Neil stood behind the colonel, positioned so they could all focus on the large central monitor. Neil glanced over and shook his head. No one else paid his arrival any mind.

Darren went straight into his office but kept the door open. He could hear his voice over the system's speakers and liked the sense of being bonded with them, this group who had shot him off to Oz and brought him home. And changed his world in the process.

When the speakers went quiet, Darren watched as Neil set his phone on the desk and touched a button. Darren knew that they were listening to his transit account, but the images that had seemed so intensely real while he spoke were now mere fragments. Like he was trying to recall a dream from weeks ago.

When his voice stopped echoing through the lab, Neil stretched and waved to Darren. Join us.

Darren walked over and drew another chair up beside Leila. He gave it a beat, then asked, 'Can I ask if my experiences have resulted in anything new?'

'You can ask anything you like,' Leila replied. 'You're one of us now.'

Alveraz remained silent, her gaze resting on the blank monitor screen.

Leila pressed, 'Isn't that right, Colonel?'

Alveraz shifted her gaze. 'What precisely do you want me to say?'

'Only what you feel ready to discuss,' Neil replied. 'We're all in this together. Isn't that right, Leila?'

It was the physicist's turn to go silent.

Neil directed his gaze to Darren. 'Back to what I said in the kitchen. Before your transit, all we could say with any certainty is that our entry point had been blocked. We were locked out. Now we have a better understanding of precisely what happened.'

'Everything you've told us fits into the big picture,' Anchali agreed.

'Your transit plays a vital role,' Leila said, watching Alveraz, her tone softly defiant. 'We understand a number of crucial elements much better now.'

'The aliens we bonded with were all intent on something else from the outset,' Neil said.

'They treat our little momentary conversation as nothing but destructive super-positioning,' Leila said. 'OK, here's another grade-school visitor, get them out of the way so we can focus on the real work. Very different to your unit.'

'We suspect the temporal displacement is different at their end,' Anchali said. 'A flash connection for us might last minutes or even hours for them.'

Alveraz rose to her feet. 'I need to check in.'

'Really, Mariana?' This from Anchali, using the colonel's first name. 'Really?'

'Stay,' Leila insisted. 'Sit.'

'We're past any objections from the higher-ups,' Neil agreed. 'Even your contact. We need to tell Darren, and you need to hear it.'

Alveraz looked at them. Really looked. Saw the determination. The grim intent, so unified it silenced her objections and forced her back down.

Neil told Darren, 'Destructive super-positioning is the scientific definition of interference. It's how we refer to the blockage we've all experienced.'

'Or barrier,' Leila said. 'Or exclusion. All of the words fit, and none of them do.'

'Except for the dissenting voices,' Anchali offered.

Neil nodded. 'Anchali's and Leila's final transits suggested at least some of them wanted to help us.' He pointed to the three whiteboards now dominated by their multicolored scrawl. 'We're desperately trying to piece together an incomplete puzzle.'

Anchali said, 'During the transits we three made, we all had the clear impression their focus was on another group. Just like you said.'

'Your description of a different civilization higher up the food chain fits precisely with our experiences,' Leila said.

'They're struggling to understand a technology that can potentially shift them to an entirely new level of existence,' Anchali said.

'Just like us,' Leila said. 'With them. Only they don't want to give us the time of day.'

'Interference,' Neil repeated. 'Connecting with us is a side product of their reaching out. Their attempts to connect with this superior race means opening up the lines of communication to us.'

'Soon as we connected and they became aware of our presence, they started to exclude us.'

'Not all of them,' Anchali corrected, pointing to the whiteboards.

'Most of them didn't want anything to do with us,' Leila insisted, bitter now. Angry. Molten in a quiet, smoldering way.

'Think about illegals at the border. Trying to slip in. Getting caught and shunted away. Our needs and hopes don't mean a thing. We're just dust in the desert. Beneath contempt.'

Anchali murmured, 'Leila. Calm yourself.'

The younger woman went silent, her dark eyes burning.

Neil said, 'We've caught very tight fragments of disagreement. Comments made to Anchali, one distinct communication with me, but mostly to Leila.'

'The one I connected with wanted to pass on information . . . something important,' Leila said, glaring at the floor by her feet. 'Two others were utterly opposed. Disgusted by the very idea.'

'I've caught faint hints of both,' Anchali said. 'Voices that merged and split apart. Then a dominant voice, a leader of some kind, stifled the argument and shut us out.'

'I'm fairly certain this dominant voice was my contact,' Neil said. 'But it's hard to be certain, because we all sensed a sort of flow that connected these four. Like they were four individuals, and then they weren't. Which makes your concept of joining—'

'It's not a concept,' Darren said. 'That's not strong enough.'

To his surprise, all of them smiled. Neil said, 'I stand corrected.'

Anchali said, 'We've needed your explanations.'

'Desperately,' Leila agreed.

'The last time I went in,' Neil said, 'this dominant voice took over and closed the door. Just shoved me away. It was a brutal moment. Like all our efforts to connect had been dismissed.'

'The same started to happen with me,' Anchali said. 'But this one entity kept communicating with Leila on her final transit. I've been trying to explain how it felt, not like I heard this, not like Leila's contact told mine.'

'They joined,' Neil said. Watching the two women. 'Just as Darren experienced. They joined, and the experience of one became that of the other.'

'Not just a memory,' Anchali agreed. 'Time isn't viewed as a one-way process there. They joined, and I lived the moment Leila's connection opened up.'

'It felt like my individual and Anchali's connection slipped through a side door together, so we could communicate,' Leila said.

'In that one instant,' Neil said, 'they passed over the foundations of a totally new mathematical formula.'

'An incredible, amazing, world-changing concept,' Anchali said.

Again, Neil pointed to the mathematical symbols covering a whiteboard and three easels. 'Observing this come even partially together stripped the breath from my body.'

'We think it's a conduit for utilizing dark energy,' Leila said.

'But it's totally and utterly incomplete.' Neil pointed to the blank whiteboards. 'We might be able to work it out. In time.'

'Time,' Leila said. Bitter. 'If only we had been granted one more communication. It just might have been enough.'

'That dominant entity discovered we were communicating,' Anchali explained. 'We were all shoved away. The experience was wrenching.'

Leila said, 'The exclusion carried a very real pain. Like the bond has been permanently severed.'

Neil said, 'These conflicting voices, they wanted to give us something. They felt a very real obligation to pass on what they knew.'

'Especially Leila's contact,' Anchali said. 'And mine, to a lesser extent. So we both tried to go back in.'

'Awful.' Leila blinked fiercely. 'After the transit, I felt like I had been forced to stare at death.'

'Mine didn't hold that level of dread,' Anchali said. 'A closed gate. Nothing more. But bad just the same.'

Tanaka spoke for the first time since Darren joined them. 'Dark energy. I know the words, and that's about it.'

Neil said, 'The human race is at a juncture. The finite limit of our energy sources, the environmental damage we cause in the quest for more, it defines us.'

'It also threatens our very existence,' Anchali said. She pointed to the glass cage. 'All of our transit experiences brought us to the same certainty. This alien civilization went through some form of existential threat. Their survival as a species, this formation of the floating city-states, came down to one thing: finding a way to tap into dark energy. If we can manage to tap into it too, humanity's survival could depend on it.'

'It makes up more than seventy percent of the universe's energy,' Neil said. 'And we can't even identify it. The only way we're certain it exists is by how it impacts the universe's expansion.'

The colonel rose, stretched, and declared, 'I need to report back to my contact. Neil, shoot me a link to everything you have.'

'On it.' He turned to Darren. 'We all agree, you should wait another day before your next transit.'

Leila said, 'Your system has gone through a very hard shock. Blood pressure through the roof, heart rate well above redline.'

'I hate to say it, but we have no idea what role age plays in recovery from such events,' Neil said.

Anchali started toward the recovery station. 'Come over here, please. I want to check your vitals.'

She took considerable care, wiring his chest and temples to the gear stationed to the gurney. She studied the readout for what to Darren felt like far too long. Then, 'Neil.'

'Yo.'

'Come here, please.'

His friend sauntered over, clearly not concerned. But as he leaned over Anchali's shoulder, he tensed. Frowned. And asked, 'Is that a blip?'

'A small one. Maybe. I'm not certain.'

Darren asked, 'Something wrong?'

Anchali continued to address Neil. 'The problem is we don't have any medical history.'

Neil straightened. Pondered. Then he turned to Darren and said, 'It's probably nothing. But it could be a slight irregularity in your heartbeat. We need to give this one more day, then take another reading before we decide.'

Darren started to protest. The desire to experience another such event was strong as hunger. But their expressions were resolute. He could tell Neil was expecting an argument, and had that rigid look to his features that took Darren straight back. As in, whatever Darren said would not budge him one inch. So Darren simply nodded acceptance and headed for his office.

* * *

Completing the DARPA files took him until late. When he finished the initial review, Darren rose, stretched, decided to go see what was on offer in the kitchen.

The three scientists remained intent on one of the whiteboards. Leila scribbled, Anchali edited, Neil stood back and frowned. Darren doubted any of them noticed his departure.

The kitchen was empty, the house quiet. Darren found a giant bowl of salad fixings on the counter. The warming oven held thinly sliced brisket. He made himself a plate and ate in weary solitude. Remembering.

Back when Gina was going through her final decline, he had grown accustomed to being felled by sudden exhaustion. In the days and nights and weeks spent at her bedside, he had learned the bitter truth about admitting defeat. As in, give in to the weariness when he could, even if he didn't want to, despite the lack of a decent spot. See to Gina's every need. Make sure she had everything possible to ease her passage through the dread hour. He couldn't save her life. So he would do what he could. Be there. For her. He had learned to sleep on floors, in chairs, even stretched over the hard benches lining hospital corridors.

He forced his legs to work and climbed the stairs and entered his bedroom. Darren stripped and used the bathroom and settled beneath the summer-weight covers. The ceiling fan pushed humid air around, not doing much to cool things down. He debated closing the window and giving into air-conditioned coolness. But the humid evening symphony was intoxicating. Palms whispered patiently, birds called back and forth, the sunset breeze shushed a constant note through the screen.

The dreamstate's arrival felt like he was already there and ready to welcome it back. Like the blissful distance was in place, and all he needed was to become aware despite being asleep. Or because of it.

Just like the previous two, this third dreamstate carried a very distinct flavor. The first had been professorial and internally focused and fixated upon time. The second was externally aimed and more clinical. Probing his connection to the here and now. Seeing it all with a new clarity.

As he came alert to this third event, the intensity became

acutely heightened. As if he was being drawn toward some unseen point, a jumping-off place, where he might actually spread wings of his own. Not just observe. Participate.

Then he realized where this dream was aimed.

He was being drawn toward his life with Gina. His lost beloved.

All the pleasure and excitement he had known previously became tainted by a flood of very real fear. Terrible wounds were about to be probed. Forcing him to make the impossible choice. Endure the dreadful, or end the exquisitely sweet release of these dreams. Because to turn away risked everything.

Then it happened.

An unguent of pure unbridled compassion poured over him. Here was healing. Or rather, here was an invitation to heal. But only if he wanted. If he was ready. To wash these wounds. Stitch them up. Move on. There was no logic to these dreamtime sensations. Yet he knew the choice was real, and his to make. He *knew* this.

Darren took the dreamtime step, and focused on what he had tried so hard to leave behind. Stepping into the life and world he had lost.

This river of healing calm carried him *backward* through events, each a logical step, each uniquely potent and yet freed from all loss, all pain, all regret.

The events formed a steady pattern moving from the here and now further and further into what was no more. The funeral led back to the moment of Gina's death. Darren saw again how he'd held her wasted body and gave all he could to ease her passage.

From there back to the hospital, then the doctors and their first nightmare prognosis. Then the weeks of tests. Her first hints of terrible distress . . .

Gone.

He knew the memories remained his forever. And the love they still shared. But the burden, the hollow void that had defined him these long and lonely months . . .

Absent.

Perhaps it would all resume once he woke. Just like it had happened the two previous times. But in that moment, he did not care. The dreamstate was enough. The release a gift, however short or long the effects remained.

The events continued their backward flight down the stream of time and memories. He was carried in incredible ease, observing a glorious vista from this dreamtime craft that powered him against time's current.

Their life together. Her father's business and how it became part of their shared days. The birth of their daughter. Their early days of married life. All the simple tenderness and caring that formed the one-ness. The redefining of who he was . . .

He woke up.

TEN

A morning breeze laced with coffee and breakfast fragrances drifted through his open window as he showered and dressed and took his time stretching. The dreamstate's lingering impact felt stronger than his current version of reality. As he opened his door and started down the upstairs corridor, he remained captured by the impossibility of leaving Gina's aching absence behind. Even if it lasted for just this one moment, the prospect of days not filled with feverish loss was almost intoxicating. Once downstairs, he opened the front door and stepped on to the porch. He breathed the scented Florida morning, reveling in the heat and the light. Gina was there with him, yet his loss was muted. Life continued. Time's onward flow was inevitable. He could accept that now. For the moment, it was enough.

As Darren re-entered the home, he decided they needed to know.

The prospect of revealing his night-time experiences filled him with a very real fear. What if secrecy was a requirement for it to happen again? What if revealing the experiences meant the portal would be permanently closed? What then?

He entered the kitchen to find everyone save Barry present. Leila and Anchali and Neil occupied one tight corner, heads almost touching as they discussed a sheet of calculations. Tanaka and the colonel stood by the rear door, cradling mugs and sharing a tight smile. Darren remarked on how similar they were, the professional soldier and his friend. Both held the ease of hunting cats. The coiled strength and tight awareness that never fully relaxed.

Neil leaned back and asked Darren, 'How are you feeling?'

'Good.' Hard as it was to expel the words, he told them, 'I've been having dreams.'

Everyone glanced over. 'It happens,' Neil said. 'Not to me. But both Leila and Anchali.'

'We assume it is the transit experience resonating at a subconscious level,' Anchali said. 'Your mind coming to terms with the impossible.'

Leila huffed. 'It didn't help, though. Did it?'

Darren saw how both women shared the same expression. Pinched with distaste or something stronger. 'You didn't like it? The dreams, I mean.'

Anchali glanced at Neil. 'Yours are pleasant?'

'Oh no. Pleasant doesn't go far enough. They were incredible. I can't begin to describe how great.'

They were all watching him now. Neil pulled out his phone, hit record. 'Try.'

So he did. Try, at least. The freedom, the intensity of a dreamtime moment of existing solely in the immediate now.

Anchali rose and gestured for Darren to seat himself. She filled a mug, opened the warming oven, and set two breakfast burritos on a plate. Darren thanked her, and watched as she resumed her seat and joined the others in studying him. Even the colonel was intensely focused on what he had to say.

Darren continued, 'My late wife, Gina, was in the hospital for almost four weeks that last time. Toward the end they started to move her into hospice care, then decided she was too weak, and the end was too close. So she remained where she was, and they made up a sort of bed for me to stay there with her. The ward nurses and one of the doctors became like distant kin, there in a quiet manner whenever I needed something, but otherwise just standing on the periphery of what had become my life. Watching. Waiting with me.'

He had never spoken of those long days, not even to his father-in-law, the man who had over time become Darren's closest friend. Now the words simply flowed. The dreamscape's peace remained with him, at least for the moment. And somehow Darren was certain they needed to know.

'After it was over, her absence defined my life,' he said. Shrugging at the inability to describe the unimaginable. 'She was gone, my world was shifted on its axis, the hollow void was simply part of my days. My every hour. Never to leave. Not ever.'

Leila's response was the most profound, at least from where

he sat. She stared at Darren with a fathomless intensity. No barriers. The woman's dark depths, the utter mystery behind her acidic rage, all exposed. She was the only one to speak. 'How could it?' she said. 'It defines who you are now.'

'But not last night, or the two nights before.' Sharing this moment with Leila, having her understand, fashioned a bond at heart level. At least for him. So he spoke to her now. No one else. 'Three times now I've been freed from all that. I reside in this . . . I don't even know how to describe it.'

'Try,' she urged. Quietly desperate. 'I want to understand.'

'I was liberated,' he said. The words felt inadequate even before they were formed. But it was all he had to go on. So he continued, 'This wasn't a return to how things were when we were together and life was good. This was here. This was now. But without the weight. I felt as if a dark lens of pain and emotions had been lifted from my mind. I saw things with a new clarity . . .' He stopped, defeated. 'I can't say it any better than that.'

Anchali leaned back. She addressed the ceiling. 'All this continues to redefine the differences between Darren's transit and our own.'

'He's been welcomed,' Neil agreed. 'We were expelled.'

Leila's gaze continued to rest on Darren. As if, for her, it remained just the two of them. Bonded.

He asked, 'How were your own dreamtime experiences?'

'Terrible,' Leila said. 'Frightening.'

'I felt invaded,' Anchali agreed.

'I was nothing more than a lab animal,' Leila said. 'A rodent who refused to stay inside my proper cage.'

'The dreams pushed at me with a pain I actually felt on a physical level,' Anchali agreed, watching Leila now. 'Like I did not deserve to live.'

'Like the transit contact wanted me to die,' Leila said. 'Painfully.'

'Like they were angry they could not kill me themselves,' Anchali agreed.

Neil demanded, 'Why am I only hearing this now?'

'We tried to tell you,' Anchali replied. 'You discounted the dreams as unimportant.'

Neil opened his mouth, clearly wanting to argue. But remained silent.

Leila said, 'My dreams were so intense I was actually glad when they shut me out and I couldn't transit again.' She glanced at Neil. 'Glad.'

Darren studied the trio, knowing their accounts represented a very real risk. He could fall asleep and descend into the nightmarish madness they had experienced. He could see the cost of their experiences stained upon their features.

Then he thought of something his father-in-law liked to say. The retired Marine one-star general, facing yet another crisis that could have potentially cost them their jobs, business, livelihoods, homes. The works. Times like these, when everything was on the line and sleep was a myth, he liked to say, *I've had a lot of traumas in my life. Most of which never happened.*

Darren told the group, 'I'm ready to go again. Yes, OK, there may or may not be an issue with my heart rate . . . What?'

He stopped mid-flow because Neil had lifted his hand. The scientist explained, 'Our equipment is fritzing.'

'That is not even close to a proper explanation,' Anchali told Darren. 'The sensors have slipped from alignment.'

'Which must be perfect,' Leila said. Still showing him that fathomless gaze. 'If you're interested in a safe transit.'

Neil offered, 'Give us a few hours. We should have identified the fritz.'

But Darren wasn't ready to let the topic go. Of course, what he was really after was an assurance it would happen again. 'What about my dreamstates?'

'Dreamstate,' Anchali said. 'Excellent.'

'Nightmare-state, more like,' Leila said.

Neil studied the two women. He noticed the phone was still recording, tapped the surface, then said, 'You've given us a good deal to consider and discuss.'

Tanaka offered, 'That's no answer.'

'It's all I have,' Neil replied. 'For the moment.'

Tanaka shrugged, told Darren, 'Finish your breakfast. It's time I introduce you to my world.'

* * *

Tanaka's Land Cruiser was creased and scratched and had a long crack along the windscreen's passenger side. But the engine purred and the tires gripped when Tanaka goosed the accelerator. He drove midway down the farm's long drive, then said, 'Best take a firm hold.' He spun the wheel and headed down a weed-infested track, little more than a game trail. They bounced around the interior like marbles.

Alveraz was seated behind the driver. As they sped along the rutted farm trail, she told Darren, 'My people have completed their preliminary check. It looks like you're going to be granted clearance.'

'As if you had any choice,' Tanaka said.

'You're not helping,' she snapped.

'Oh, excuse me. Is that my role here? Play your backup?' Tanaka shot her a tight smile. 'Sorry, I missed that memo.'

Alveraz told Darren, 'Any student of history will tell you, the current status quo we live in is a rare thing. Holding on to this level of non-combat is temporary. I won't call it peace. Conflict remains part of the reality too many are enduring. Even so, there are boundaries to these clashes. The threats remain contained. And it all comes down to maintaining a balance of power.'

They bounced and rattled through acres of orange grove, then entered a section that had been left in its pristine old-growth state. The track smoothed as Tanaka wound between live oaks and wild palms. The place took Darren straight back. Florida's first natives called such areas hammocks, a stretch of elevated hard earth that offered sanctuary during the heaviest of storms.

Tanaka entered the central clearing and halted between a trio of square tents. Two ATVs were parked to Darren's left. A young woman pushed through the middle tent's entrance-netting and walked over. She wore a tank top, cutoffs and boots. Her dark hair was chopped into uneven lengths and streaked pink. Tattoos covered both arms, legs, shoulders, neck. She pushed dark shades on to her hair, revealing hard eyes. 'What's up?'

'Just giving the new recruit a tour,' Tanaka said. 'Darren, this is Mora.'

She checked out Darren, then nodded to Alveraz. 'Soldier lady.'

'Everything good?'

'Five by five.'

Alveraz asked, 'You need anything?'

'Better cellphone service, booze, portable PlayStation, hot shower, fresh steaks, spa day.'

Alveraz replied, 'You're on duty, soldier.'

'Wrong on multiple counts. You're the only soldier, and I work nobody's hours but my own.' Just the same, Mora stuck her hand through the rear window, bumped fists with the colonel. 'Jimmy and the Tank are on patrol. You want me to call them in?'

'No, we're not staying. You're keeping a close watch on the skies?'

She pointed back to her tent. 'Twenty-four seven. Nothing since that flyby last night.'

Alveraz said, 'Describe that.'

'I told you already. Twice.' When the colonel remained silent, Mora gave her a pained expression and said, 'Little after two. Tank had just come on duty. Whatever it was zipped past. Bang and gone. Too fast for a bird, too low for a plane. I was still awake and I thought I heard a buzz.'

Alveraz came to full alert. 'You didn't tell me that before.'

'Just thought of it.' Mora shrugged. 'I kinda figured it for a bug, nightbird. I was half asleep. Then Tank came in and said something just streaked across his screen. So I called.'

Alveraz asked, 'Did it fly over the compound?'

Mora nodded. 'Right above the warehouse. Why we decided it was worth an alert.'

Alveraz stared straight ahead, thinking. Finally she nodded and said, 'Tell Tank he did good.'

Tanaka did the fist-bump thing, said, 'Stay in touch.' Once he turned the pickup around and they were headed back down the trail, he asked Alveraz, 'Are you going to report this?'

Alveraz kept staring at the sunlit fields.

Tanaka drove slowly enough to observe her in the rearview mirror. 'I believe somebody mentioned that as being part of your remit.'

'Say I do.' The colonel addressed the window. 'Imagine for a moment I run this up the chain of command, and not just alert my primary contact. It means everything that's happening here suddenly becomes official. Washington will take charge of oversight. And this operation would be shifted to somewhere under tighter control. My guess would be one of the structures inside the Andrews Air Base secure zone. With their staff running the show.'

'Neil would freak,' Tanaka said. 'He'd drop tools and bolt for the corporate life.'

'Not just Neil,' Alveraz agreed. 'Imagine the good doctor Leila working under some Pentagon bureaucrat's direct supervision.'

'Not happening. Not in a billion years,' Tanaka said. 'So, no report.'

'Not unless it happens again.' Alveraz sighed her way around. 'Which it probably will. I feel it in my bones.'

As Tanaka retraced his way along the same rutted trail, she asked, 'Where was I?'

'Balance of power,' Tanaka replied.

She shifted to address Darren. 'To the outsider, the non-combatant, the individuals blinded by the luxury of living in safety, those words are something they read in the paper. To an officer serving on the nation's front line, balance of power is how we maintain our nation's tenuous hold on peace.'

They reached the main drive and headed out, away from the farmhouse and the concrete monolith of mystery. Darren studied his old friend, the knotted muscles, the scars over his knuckles, the singular intensity that had always defined Tanaka. Darren thought their two-on-one lecture bordered on overkill. But all he said was, 'You think Neil's work may threaten the status quo?'

'The sheer potential of second sound, what it represents, is mind-bending,' Alveraz said.

Darren hesitated, then asked, 'Is that all we're talking about?'

Alveraz replied slowly, 'As far as everyone and everywhere outside the compound, yes. Only my primary contact knows about the transits. She exists totally outside the official power structure. You understand?'

Darren thought the colonel could not have made the message any clearer if she'd used a hammer. 'Yes.'

'Neil is coming at the quantum mysteries in a totally new direction,' Tanaka said. 'If the corporate world ever caught wind of his work, they'd become Neil's opposition. And if that happens, as soon as they realize they can't throw money at it and catch up in a hurry, they'd go on the attack.'

The colonel said, 'Tell me you understand why we're having this conversation.'

Alveraz reminded Darren of irritating hours in his former life, dealing with federal bureaucrats who entered his company looking for a reason to say no. Turn them down. Spending every chance they had to lecture him on the ins and outs of federal contracts. Acting like they were the only people on earth who understood how things worked. How he was incapable of making it through the day without their overbearing lectures.

'I'm waiting,' Alveraz snapped.

Darren wondered if the colonel ever allowed herself to become a bit more feminine, perhaps even vulnerable. 'I dislike being lectured to like I was some raw recruit.'

Alveraz said, 'That's not—'

'I've spent the past thirty years building a company from nothing. Working in a highly competitive field, beating out global corporations with much deeper pockets. Dealing with Pentagon-style bullies on a daily basis. Being forced to endure lectures about the blindingly obvious. Tell me you understand what I'm saying.'

Alveraz leaned back. Silent.

'You want me to remain alert. Fine. You want me to tell you if I notice anything out of the ordinary. No problem. Is that it? Are we done now?' He faced forward and pretended to settle. 'Good. I'm so glad we had this little chat.'

Titusville had grown considerably in the thirty-three years since Darren's last visit. Just the same, what he saw left him with the distinct impression that very little had changed. The town was home to well-paid blue-collar NASA technicians and engineers. Ditto for factory workers serving any number of industries lining the interstate. Which included the largest three armament makers in Florida. Titusville had a well-earned reputation as the place to go for guns, drugs and trouble.

Part of Titusville's problem was that it had no permanent beach access. Their only way across the intracoastal was via the Max

Brewer Bridge, which was built and maintained by NASA. This granted the federal bureaucracy the right to close it any time they wished. NASA restricted bridge access to authorized personnel for all launches, and days leading up to said events, and pretty much any other time they felt a need or inclination to shut it down. Without warning. No explanation given. Ever.

The barrier island itself was gorgeous, a pristine stretch of wildlife preserves, national parks and the stunningly beautiful Playalinda Beach. Twenty miles of shoreline, no hotels, no towns, no crowds, nada. Great when visitors were granted access. Infuriating when not.

They passed through Titusville's newly redeveloped business district, with brick walkways and artistically designed streetlights and sparkling shopfronts. Well-heeled pedestrians strolled past blooming mini-parks and late-model vehicles.

Tanaka turned away from the waterfront and headed inland. Gradually the neighborhoods turned grim. Shadows sprouted, so strong they defied the Florida sunlight. Gang graffiti tagged houses. Plywood replaced broken windows. Condemned signs sprouted from unkempt yards.

They turned a corner, and instantly Darren knew they had arrived.

The martial arts studio took up an entire block. Two young people wearing more gang tats than clothes stood on both corners. They offered Tanaka a two-fingered wave as he parked. In contrast to the other blocks, all the neighboring houses were neat, freshly painted, safe.

There were three structures – a residence, a dorm and a third house that had been hollowed out and refashioned into an open-fronted dojo. Three young people tended the gardens, another two raked the sandpits holding three makiwara training poles. A dozen or so people trained with bōjutsu fighting sticks. An older woman in black tank top and traditional gi training pants and cloth slippers stood with arms crossed, calling out instructions.

Tanaka rose from the pickup, motioned for Darren to join him. Alveraz opened her door but remained seated, watching.

Darren's oldest friend approached the woman, accepted her kiss and swift embrace. The woman then spoke a single word.

Instantly the trainees halted and straightened and stood breathing hard. Tanaka walked her back, said, 'Darren, this is my wife, Orna.'

She was not tall, the top of her head scarcely reaching Tanaka's shoulder. Just the same, Darren had the feeling he looked up at her. She studied Darren, her gaze steady and so intense he felt stripped to the bone. Finally she touched his upper arm. 'Let's walk.'

Her hair was a raven and silver mane, her eyes wild with an untamed fire. The youth on corner duty offered a quick half-bow as they passed. Orna gave no sign she even noticed, and yet when they had walked another few paces she said, 'Life sings in these young friends. A ferocious roar of song. I wish you could hear just how precious their spirit voices sound to me. And to my husband. Who counts you among his closest and dearest friends.'

Darren had no idea how to respond. Nor did he think she actually expected him to speak. He walked and listened and felt all the missing years be knitted back together. Here in this woman with her softly lilting speech was the story of who Tanaka had become, and why.

'The problem is the heart's melody sung by these young students does not fit this world. They have been shaped by events so harsh and terrible it makes you weep. To others their song is just noise. Screeching, loud, angry, threatening, dangerous.' She gestured behind them. 'Here, we show them it is all right to sing. Here, in our refuge, their melody is welcome. Others see hardcore losers battling out their rage. Such outsiders are afraid of what they find here. Tanaka and I, we see an orchestra in the making. We are filled with hope.'

She was a rare woman, a fierce vixen whose every motion and word spoke of warrior queens and bygone eras. Colonel Mariana Alveraz was a military officer to her bones. Tanaka's wife was something else entirely. She would never fit inside anyone's army, no matter how grand the cause. Orna was one of a kind. A force of nature, born to fill others with the rare gift of destiny. She told him, 'You left, and in leaving you tore the soul from your friendship. No one recognized your role until they had cast you away.'

Darren saw and listened, but mostly he felt. And what he felt was the need to say, 'Neil told me they were jealous.'

'Perhaps. Even probably. But does it matter?'

'Not so much. Not anymore.'

She offered him an approving smile. 'You have grown. And so have they. It was how they filled the vacuum of your absence.'

When they turned back, Darren saw that Tanaka had taken up station by one of the combat-training poles. He made slow motion attack moves, watched by half a dozen students in pristine white gis. Orna continued, 'The four children you once were, the reckless young men you grew into, these people are no more. Your departure woke them from their adolescent slumber. They are independent spirits now, and yet still you remain bound together. Even you, is that not so?'

Darren listened to the woman's melody continue even in the silence, and felt no need to respond.

'The vows you made to a good woman and her clan, that page of your adult saga has drawn to a close. And though it may not seem so in this hard moment, you will heal. You will begin anew. Tanaka was right. You, my husband's oldest friend, are strong enough to recover from even this dark night.'

Darren started to correct her, then decided it was best to remain silent. He liked her gift of comfort, no matter how badly misplaced.

'The question you must face is what next? Because the time of choice is upon you all. They only see brief glimpses, faint whispers upon the midnight wind, nothing more. This forms the true purpose behind why they called you back. They could not name the reason, it was just a feeling, and I saw no need to explain. But you sense it already, as do I. It wasn't just to work through the forms. You are to point the way ahead. If you will.'

They stopped there in the middle of the otherwise empty street. Lit by more than heat and sun. 'Here is why we needed to speak, you and I. So that you can see clearly the need to decide. How will your life's next pages be written? With ease and the caring comfort of family and friends? Blind to the mortal danger of a cause that is not your own?'

The fire in her dark green gaze was so intense it almost hurt.

And yet there also burned a spark that threatened to reawaken him from recent loss. Darren found himself frightened and attracted both. He breathed around the conflict, mouth open, great heaving searches for air.

'You see time's unrelenting hand poised upon your life's final chapters. You hear a faint melody drifting in, the song of invitation. A few last lines of life's poetry. So brilliant they might transform the saga of your days on earth. Shine with a splendor so brilliant, it may well carry your name and those of your friends into the myths of generations yet unborn. If you are willing.' She nodded to his silence, as if in genuine approval. 'It is your choice. Your power. Your gift.'

ELEVEN

When they left the dojo, Darren took the rear seat so he could remain immersed in Orna's words. Arguing with her now that the woman was no longer present, saying what would not have been possible in her presence. Long after the words themselves faded, he still felt bonded to her remarkable intensity. No matter how misguided her confidence in him and his potential might have been.

Tanaka stopped at a taco stand, where a bearded man in a stained apron stepped from the van to embrace him. The chef's place was taken by a heavyset woman, then by two younger women.

'He tried to save their nephew from the gangs,' Alveraz said. 'He failed.'

'Tanaka's wife is . . .' Darren sought a proper word, something that might contain a shred of the sentiments and conflict. He could not find the proper term, and in the end left the sentence unfinished.

Alveraz understood, nonetheless. 'Orna doesn't want Tanaka to transit. She feels it might endanger what they're accomplishing here.'

What Darren thought was Orna was one lady he never wanted to argue with. All he said was, 'Makes sense.'

'He wants to, though. Very much.'

'What about you?'

Mariana Alveraz waited until Tanaka returned with their meals, three tacos for each of them – grilled mahi with piquant sauce, pulled pork, and the truck's specialty, pollo guisado. A few bites in, Alveraz replied, 'I'm not sure that would be wise. A military lifer going on an interplanetary mission.'

Tanaka swung around, the pickup's central console broad enough to hold both their meals. 'Guess that rules me out too.'

'You're a man of peace who fights to protect,' she replied. 'I've spent my life studying battle tactics and war games.'

'Kata fighting routines,' he countered. 'Bōjutsu. Kendo. Kenjutsu.'

She did not respond.

'It would shut Leila up,' Tanaka said. 'You taking the plunge.'

'It would certainly be something,' Alveraz said. 'Silencing that woman.'

Darren waited until they had finished eating to tell Alveraz, 'I owe you an apology for speaking like I did earlier. You were trying to bring me up to speed. What I heard was all the frustrating trivialities of a thousand earlier conversations.' He hesitated, then decided to add, 'Plus I'm still feeling off. Like I'm mentally disjointed. At least partly.'

Alveraz asked, 'The transit?'

'No. Well, at least not directly. Those dreams I talked about over breakfast, they're impacting me on a very deep level.'

Alveraz asked, 'You're certain they're related to your transit?'

'At first I wasn't sure. Now, I think, yes. Definitely a connection. Maybe something more.'

Tanaka said, 'The ladies described having terrible nightmares. Leila sounded convinced they're somehow part of the overall transit experience.'

'They sound similar. But mine are definitely not bad.' A breath, then, 'Like I told the others, I'd actually call them wonderful.'

Tanaka said, 'Neil discounts them as subconscious aftereffects.'

Alveraz replied, 'Maybe so. But he needs to keep a record.' To Darren, 'Does he?'

'He recorded our conversation this morning. But I had the impression this was a first. And to be clear, this has not been a singular event.'

'Tell Neil I said this needs to become part of his remit.'

'All right.'

Tanaka started the car, waved a farewell to the family, and pulled into traffic. 'Neil probably doesn't want to include dreams because of the possible blowback.'

'Transiting to an alien world – we don't even know where it's located – slipping inside the consciousness of beings we can't describe.' Alveraz spoke to her side window. 'Coming back with data that could totally upend our entire civilization. What's the matter with adding a few bad dreams to the mix?'

Darren started to remind her that his own dreams were far from bad, but decided in the end to simply ask, 'The flyby Mora mentioned. Is someone spying on us?'

'One incident isn't enough to assume anything definite,' she replied. 'They didn't hover, they didn't approach.'

Tanaka said, 'Photographing the terrain wouldn't take long. Quick flyover, fast high-dev camera sweeping the terrain, finish.'

'Thank you ever so very much not at all,' she replied. 'As if I needed another reason to lose sleep.'

Darren asked, 'Another incident?'

In the silence that followed, Darren sensed jagged fragments forming a semblance of clarity. OK, maybe not all of them. But some. Barry's phone call and the tense, nearly desperate way he had asked Darren to come. Clearing Neil out of NASA. The farmhouse in the middle of Florida nowhere-land. The huge pile of funds and equipment Darren was organizing into a decent paper-flow. The colonel assigned to hover like a human vulture over their every move. Tanaka's crew on patrol.

Darren guessed, 'Somebody's been caught spying?'

'Not exactly.' Tanaka rewarded him with a single glance in the rearview mirror, his eyes crimped with what might have passed for a smile. He told Alveraz, 'Darren needs to know.'

'The NSA monitors traffic between NASA and outside contractors,' Alveraz said. 'DARPA requested an alert if anything mentioned Neil's work. They received a red flag last week.'

'We suspect it was either a NASA engineer or someone working at the Pentagon,' Tanaka said. 'The Cape is going through a series of major cutbacks. All it takes is one mid-level specialist who gets the chance to pay off the credit card debt. Just keep his corporate friends informed about what they're doing over there in Canaveral's building nineteen.'

'That happens more often than we'd like to admit,' Alveraz said.

'And we're fairly certain that isn't the first time information has been passed to the corporate opposition,' Tanaka said. To Alveraz, 'Tell him the rest.'

Alveraz said, 'Two weeks ago, Leila was accosted outside her favorite bar.'

'Standing by the rear door, enjoying a quiet smoke,' Tanaka said.

'What the so-called thugs didn't know was, she's been studying martial arts under your friend here,' Alveraz said.

'Leila started long before we met.' Tanaka's smile was real now. Hungry. 'Just took those two apart was all she did.'

Darren thought the timing placed it right around Barry's call, telling Darren it was urgent he make the trip.

Alveraz said, 'No ID on them, driving a stolen vehicle, carrying unregistered firearms, and something else.'

'Military-style pneumatic syringes,' Tanaka said. 'Filled with this nasty brew.'

Darren could see the colonel's warning there in her gaze. *Better you don't know.* He was about to respond when the roar came out of nowhere.

The huge, ravenous bellow was aimed straight for Alveraz's side of their vehicle.

The volume grew louder still, presaging destruction.

The shock catapulted him mentally away from all sensations except sound. The engine's roar was replaced by wrenching metal. Shattering glass. A scream, perhaps from the pickup's mortally wounded engine. Then another shriek, this one definitely female in origin.

Darren was hammered on his right side as the door leaped inward and the seat crumpled. Side airbags punched him from both sides. The seat rose up and gripped him as tight as an upholstered fist.

He fought for breath, trapped anew by the sudden onset of multiple pains.

Then, thankfully, he passed out.

TWELVE

There definitely should not have been another dreamstate. Not then, lying in the hospital bed, linked to drips and beeping machines, filled with some drug so potent it rendered his circulation slow as a half-melted ice flow. Just the same, it happened.

The shift to dreamstate awareness carried an almost audible snap. He simply came to full alert, drawn from the drugged depths in the space of a single heartbeat. Faster.

Analysis was the focal point to this dream encounter. The drive to delve deeply, identify core elements, draw tentative conclusions, seek evidence to prove or disprove . . . All while asleep, drugged, dreaming.

There was a lumbering force to this latest event, one strong enough to shove its way through the drugs. Like an elephant plodding about the place, trunk swinging. The hunger to study and analyze dominated everything. He felt a keen awareness, stronger than anything he had known previously. In this particular dreamstate, it was everything. The ability to seek, analyze, deduce, this was life at its fullest. For the first time, he could fathom the forces that had directed Neil's entire life. The quest for quest's sake. A professional hunter, seeking to expand and redefine scientific boundaries.

The dreamstate's awareness swiveled around and glanced back at his own life. Again, the inspection carried a total newness, as if he had never spent a single instant studying his days. In this moment, he viewed his existence as defined by the safety of numbers and spreadsheets and federal forms. All this was fine. But only so long as he served the greater purpose. Here in this brief, redefining instant, he saw the true purpose to his return to Florida and these most recent days. His goal, the purpose driving him forward, was to form a concrete structure in which the scientists could safely work. This message or viewpoint was branded into his bruised and fragile state, then the awareness turned away.

His boundaries expanded far enough to become mindful of his physical body, the needle in his left arm, the slow regular heartbeat, the inflamed tendons, the bandage on his head ... There followed a very strange moment, almost as if he fought against himself, struggling to fathom the injuries, his drugged state, the way his eyelids refused to open, the strange odors drawn with each tiny breath. He felt enormously confused by all this. A worrying moment of indecision, as if inside this dreamstate he was able to ask the impossible question: did he want to live here? Did he want to exist at all?

The dreamstate vanished.

There was none of the gradual return, nor any lingering distance that flavored his awakening this time. Instead, the lumbering beast of pure analytic force thrust outward and was away.

Darren felt as though he screamed himself awake.

He managed a tea-kettle's hiss, nothing more. In the instant before Darren opened his eyes, he had a fleeting impression of time's fabric being torn asunder. That in fact he was granted the ability to peer around the corner, and see what was headed their way.

Shame his vision remained so foggy.

Just the same, as Darren listened to his silent shriek fade to nothingness, he found himself steadied. A brief glimpse of the way ahead, no matter how vague, offered an assurance that he was ready to face whatever awaited him.

He took a steadying breath, hoping against all logic that it was indeed the case, and not simply the combination of his dreamstate and whatever drug that kept his pains at a comfortable distance.

Then he opened his eyes.

Leila was seated beside his bed, her face stained by tears she had shed hours ago. Perhaps longer. Darren un-gummed his lips and mouthed the word, water. She used the controls to lift the back of his bed, then hefted a plastic cup and held it while he pulled on the straw. Darren drank, breathed, drank again.

When he nodded, she replaced the cup and said, 'Mariana is in a very bad way.'

Darren found himself mostly caught by how broken she sounded. That and how the scream he'd heard now had a name. 'Will she . . .'

'A life without full mobility, for Mariana, is no life.' She cuffed her eyes, impatient with her own weakness. 'Full throttle ahead, that defines Mariana.'

'I thought you . . .'

'Detested her? Yes and no.' She sniffed loudly. 'We fought mainly because we're so alike.'

He reached for the cup and took genuine pleasure in accomplishing that simple act. His internal complaints were made much louder by moving. He drank, using the time for a quick inspection. Ribs, pain. Ditto for his right arm. Shoulder worse, and bandaged in a way that suggested either a break or dislocation. Ditto for the way his head was strapped. Hip, yeah, pain there too. And his right thigh.

Other than that, he was OK.

He was alive. He was healthy enough that Leila sat beside him and spoke only about a patient in another room. For the moment, that was enough.

If it had been up to him, Darren would have preferred to be up and mobile before getting hit with Mariana's status. But Leila did not offer him that chance. She launched straight in, the telling releasing new tears. 'Her brain is swollen and they've induced a coma in the hope her conditions will improve. The ligaments to her upper spine are so inflamed they can't tell for certain if she's suffered any nerve damage.'

He asked because he had to. 'Tanaka?'

'OK. Bruised.' She waved a hand, her fingers glistening with uncommon tears. 'Marginally better than you.'

'Do you know what happened?'

She offered a marginal shrug. 'You were struck by something called a Dodge Mega Cab. Big, heavy, powerful. Witnesses claim two men started toward Tanaka's ride with guns drawn. But the police were only a block or so away. They escaped by way of another vehicle. You're lucky to be alive.'

Darren breathed around the enormity of being here. Safe. Alive. 'Where's Neil?'

'With Mariana. He asked me to be here when you woke up.' She wiped her face. 'As if that can help anything.'

Despite the circumstances, it felt good to smile. He could well imagine Neil gently telling this woman to go away. 'And Anchali?'

She glared at him through the tears. 'We're talking about Mariana.'

'Of course we—'

'Who is as close to death's door as possible while still breathing.' The need to argue, the heat, was back in her gaze. 'And breathing only because the doctors won't let her stop.'

'I understand.' Darren spoke to her as he would his daughter, back in those fairly awful teenage rebellions. As if nothing could possibly touch him. He spread the words out, calm as a clinician. 'Leila, where is Anchali?'

'With Neil. Of course.'

Darren lay back. Gathering himself against the onslaught of pain. He could feel the medical veil begin to give. 'Tell them we need to meet. While there's still time.'

Her anger was taking control now. 'Your injuries are no more serious than a scratch on your ego.'

'Listen to me.' He felt as removed from her ire as he had from the screaming matches between his late wife and their unruly daughter. 'This is vital. We need—'

She did not rise so much as bounce. 'I thought you were almost becoming a friend.'

He lay and watched her storm out. Leila did her best to slam the door, but the pneumatic hinges defied her. Darren reached for the buzzer, pressed twice, then settled back. It felt good to smile despite the incoming distress. Leila really could take a few lessons from his daughter on throwing a decent tantrum.

The nurse appeared, and responded to his smile with one of her own. 'You rang?'

'My head hurts.'

'Well, that's not surprising, is it. Seeing as how you used it to open a car window.'

'Can I have something for the pain?'

'You're not due for more meds until six. But I've always had a soft spot for men with nice eyes. Let me see what we can do.' She walked to the small apparatus on his bedside table, inspected the digital timer, then asked, 'On a scale of one to ten, what's your current distress level?'

'Right this instant, eight and a half. But what I feel headed my way, ten doesn't go far enough.'

'That does it, then.' She tapped the ID strung from her neck on the machine's electric eye, which gave off an agreeable peep in response. She pressed a button, did so once more, then asked, 'How's that?'

The water's icy wash had nothing on this. 'Wow.'

'And that's the right answer.' She pressed it a third time, then straightened and gripped his wrist. She checked her watch against his pulse, then watched his eyelids begin sinking. 'I do believe this particular train is leaving the station.'

Darren wanted to tell her how important it was to be back and cogent before too long. But like the nurse said, he was already gone.

The great lumbering beast of pure force was there waiting for Darren's return.

In that first instant of dreamstate awareness, Darren realized the true cost of his exquisite release. Perhaps he had always known, yet somehow managed to remain willfully blind. Even now, as he saw the truth in raw detail, he wanted to shrug it off. The cost was insignificant. He did not simply accept the joyous moment, freed from all burdens. He dove straight in.

Even though this momentary freedom was possible only when he shared his life with an alien entity.

Just like now.

His knee-jerk response was so what? They were joined together on the other end, so why not here?

Darren sensed a faint whisper of internal protest. Some discordant note. A warning.

His reaction was the same. So what? And he gave in to the incredible awareness of now.

That very instant, almost before the acceptance was formed, off they went. These two temporary allies started a disembodied trek through the hospital.

The unique newness of everything Darren saw had a reason now. Slipping from his body, passing through the closed door, sweeping down the corridor and into another room holding his friends. Only now what he observed was a chamber where two women and a dark-skinned male, all scientists, were joined by a wheelchair-bound individual as they clustered around a fifth individual who lay immobile on a hospital bed. Darren and his temporary mate wondered why they were there at all, helplessly gathered around someone they could not do anything for, instead of continuing their vital search for answers. What were tears? What indeed made three of them feminine?

There was no time for answers, nor any real interest. Marking the moment with valid questions was enough.

Just like a scientist, Darren thought, as they left the room and returned to the corridor. Drifting. Studying.

This marked his first hospital visit since witnessing his wife's final breath. The difference could not possibly have been greater. Darren reveled in being the emotionless observer. The intensity of analysis generated by his visitor was simply part of this particular dreamstate's joy. Together with his alien guest, Darren witnessed how humans dealt with the mystery of illness. Past the nurses' station, through a crowd of students accompanying a consultant.

Into a surgical ward.

Darren felt an extreme shock as the anesthetized patient was sliced open. For the first time ever inside a dreamstate, the jolt of horror split him from the alien scientist. A surgeon delved inside a patient's body, repairing an improperly functioning component, drawing out an element of disease and the errors it caused . . .

The revelation of human frailty, witnessing the risks involved in this definition of life, wrenched them apart.

His final thought before opening his eyes was, *Welcome to my world.*

Darren woke to find a nurse checking his vitals. He accepted her offer of food, allowed her to raise him to a seated position, then sat observing the day. His sunlit window was etched with a quantum light. A brilliance only he could see. Darren watched the morning sun slowly write the script of another day, and felt a building awareness of what needed doing.

The dreamscape's force had departed with his visitor. For once, he did not mind its passage. Darren had spent his entire professional career hunting out the next step. How to grow a small air-taxi service into a regional operation. His wife's family handled the actual planes. His business was strategy. And he was good at his job. So good, in fact, they challenged the regional giants and were rewarded with a buyout.

That was what this moment required. Strategy. Developing a plan. Searching out what needed doing brought its own force, one so potent his body hummed.

His meal done, the nurse helped him rise and stagger to the bathroom. Showering was both taxing and wonderful. He shaved and dressed in clothes laid out on a plastic stool he was tempted to use while bathing, but in the end forced himself to remain erect. He emerged wearing a cloud-soft cotton shirt and shorts held up by an elastic waistband, perfect items for a man negotiating his new independence. And there waiting for him was Tanaka seated in a wheelchair. Darren greeted him with, 'I guess your years of training paid off.'

'Not training. Just luck.' Tanaka came close to smiling. 'It is very good to see you mobile.'

Darren plucked at his shirt. 'These are yours?'

'Orna brought them. I'm glad they fit.' He rose and gestured to the wheelchair. 'The others are waiting.'

'Good. I have an idea. And we need to talk before I zone out again.'

'Correction, kohai. You talk, they listen, neh?' He indicated the chair. 'You sit, I push.'

'I can walk.'

'Walking is for another day.' Tanaka rolled the chair over. 'Besides, I need to lean on something. It might as well be you.' Tanaka held the chair steady while he lowered himself, then told him, 'The nurse stopped by and said it's time for your meds.'

'I'd rather wait until we're done.' Despite the complaints from multiple joints and his head, it felt beyond good to be freed from his prone position. Darren could feel the healing process at work, a brief glimpse into what lay ahead. Healing. Mobility. Tomorrow.

When they emerged from the room, a nurse tried to take control of Darren's chair. Tanaka responded with an immensely polite negative, the iron will clear in his tone. The nurse monitored their progress a few more paces, then walked away.

It seemed right to gather around Mariana's inert form. Darren accepted Anchali's embrace, a gentle moment with Barry and then Neil resting their hands on Darren's shoulder, a wounded glance from Leila. At least the young woman remained silent. They took up position, Leila seated on the bed and holding Mariana's limp fingers, Tanaka resting in the room's only chair, Neil stationed on the wall behind Tanaka's chair, Anchali and Barry positioned to either side of the window. Darren shifted one wheel slightly so Mariana's pale features were not directly in his line of sight, and launched straight in. 'I think we should treat this as our one and only chance to prepare, and be certain we're not overheard.'

Neil said, 'You have a plan?'

'It's our duty to make the plan, not Darren's,' Tanaka corrected. 'The sensei's task is to point the direction.'

Leila straightened. 'You actually called him that? Sensei?'

Tanaka said, 'Go on, Darren.'

'The question we need to focus on is, why attack us? Why there?' Darren waited. When no one responded, he went on: 'The only answer I can come up with is they were after Mariana. They wanted to take her out.'

'Makes sense,' Barry said. 'They can insert a spy now. No question.'

Neil asked, 'Who is "they"?'

'Wrong question,' Tanaka said.

Barry responded anyway. 'The police don't have a suspect. The car was stolen, the driver and second man fled the scene. The police have taken images from nearby security cameras and are searching databases—'

'Wrong answer,' Tanaka said.

'In the long run, all this is important,' Darren said. 'And we need to keep track of anything they discover. But right now it's secondary. From this moment, the instant we leave this room, our work is split in two. All our discussions, all the data, all the work, is focused on just one aim.'

'Second sound,' Anchali said. 'Harmonic communication. Exploring the possibilities our new communication system in space offers.'

Neil said, 'That's as much as our backers will know. But we need to include dark energy as a component of the veil.'

Anchali nodded. 'Whoever they insert in Mariana's place, one glance at our whiteboards and they'll know what we're chasing.'

Leila said, 'So soon as we're back, we erase the work.'

Tanaka shook his head. 'Probably too late for that.'

'I agree,' Neil said. 'And to deny it after they've viewed our work would only raise suspicions.'

Darren asked, 'Is there any chance you could convince DARPA that your dark energy calculations are derived from the work on second sound?'

In response, Anchali and Neil looked at Leila. Darren could see the woman wanted to fight, argue, contradict. Instead she looked at Mariana, thought, and decided, 'It's a stretch. But yes. We could make that argument.'

Barry asked, 'Does that risk having your work stolen by whoever was behind this attack?'

All three scientists shook their heads.

'Good luck with that,' Neil said.

'We're trapped in a storm of unconnected fragments,' Anchali said.

'So that is it,' Darren said. 'The task everyone focuses on is second sound.'

Leila asked, 'Including you?'

'All my costings, all the work anyone is able to see, second sound has been the key element,' Darren replied. 'Now we need to decide on what we show the watchers. What is the huge question that justifies our being set apart like this.'

'Actually, it's several questions,' Neil said, his eyes sparking now. 'We need to build a stable link so the ability to send and receive becomes constant, like using a sat phone.'

'Miniaturizing the equipment required to send a message,' Leila offered. 'Absolutely crucial.'

'Not to mention defining a clear link between second sound and dark energy,' Anchali offered. 'Which is crucial if we want to hide the true source of our new equations.'

'Which will demand weeks of work,' Leila said. 'Attempting the impossible.'

'The job of every good theoretical physicist,' Neil said. 'Right, Leila?'

'And this grants us a chance to continue with the other project,' Darren said. And waited.

Leila snapped, 'It's futile even discussing this. We're all shut out, remember?'

Tanaka smiled.

Darren said, 'Not all of us.'

Barry said, 'Well now.'

Darren asked, 'How many know I managed the transit, or whatever you want to call it?'

'Transit still works for me,' Neil said.

Darren went on: 'Mariana knows. Would she have already told DARPA about my transit?'

'No,' Tanaka said. 'Absolutely not.'

Leila was too cross to simply let it go. 'You're guessing.'

'On the drive before we were attacked, she said she was holding back,' Darren recalled.

Tanaka added, 'Mariana's remit was to immediately report every development. But up to now, she has said nothing about *any* successful transit to her direct superiors. Only to a single trustworthy contact.'

Leila did not respond.

Anchali offered, 'Mariana pressed her superiors to clear Darren officially, have him fully included as part of our team. She based this on real work done by a real accountant with experience in real federal procurements.' Anchali offered the inert figure a sorrowful glance. 'She said nothing more because she didn't need to.'

Darren waited through the silence. Liking how they were moving together now. Even Leila.

Finally Neil asked, 'You have an idea how we should proceed?'

'On the level of secrets,' Anchali added, watching Leila. 'Walking the dark path. Together.'

'My transits,' Darren replied. 'We amp them up. Increase the number.'

'This isn't about just maintaining a connection,' Neil said.

'We've been left with only half a formula. Not to mention how your body verges on the broken.'

Darren's pain formed an incoming wave. Out there on the horizon, sweeping in, soon to obliterate his ability to form coherent thought. He knew they needed to hear it all. But not now. His sole focus was to maintain a calm mask. Show them he was ready to go back. Transit. Despite everything. He replied, 'My body isn't the part making the transit.'

'He has a point,' Tanaka said.

'But your heart,' Neil protested. 'The strain.'

'Basically, the same response,' Darren said. 'My heart wasn't damaged.'

'You don't know that.'

'Actually, we do,' Anchali said. 'He's been on the heart monitor since his arrival.'

Neil shot her a look. 'You're not helping.'

'Right now, I'm the only transit connection you have,' Darren said. 'And something else. I know you discount the whole issue of these dreamstates. But through them I've maintained a safe connection. Remember what I told you after that first transit. They want me there.'

Tanaka said, 'Mariana thought these dreamstates were an issue that needed serious consideration.'

Neil demanded, 'How many of these dreamstates have you had?'

'Five.'

'I still don't . . .' Neil stopped because Leila was on her feet and headed for the door.

'We can talk this to death and nothing's going to change.' She motioned to the group. 'Darren's idea is the only one on the table.' When no one moved, she snapped, 'Let's go, people. Ticking clock, remember?'

THIRTEEN

Darren drifted through much of the forty-eight-minute drive back from the hospital. He traveled in the front seat because tilting it back removed some of the strain from his bruised hip. Leila drove, with Neil and Anchali seated behind. Barry had been called away by yet another urgent issue, and would join them later. Tanaka remained at the hospital, to share watching over Mariana with his wife and team. Darren feared that returning to the farmhouse would shatter his fragile sense of confidence. Instead, when they wound their way down the final stretch and the compound came into view, everything snapped into focus.

A chalk-blue Equinox with USAF insignia on the doors was parked by the satellite dishes. When Leila pulled up alongside and cut the motor, Darren said, 'Nothing's changed.'

As Leila swung around, Anchali said, 'I agree.'

'Oh, really.' Even now, Leila's former heat was gone. 'Then please enlighten the rest of us.'

Darren found himself reassured by the woman's relative calm. 'Everything we discussed, all we do that is visible to the outside world, is just a smokescreen.'

'A veil,' Anchali agreed. 'Important, but also insignificant.'

'Whoever is waiting for us inside,' Darren said. 'All they are is . . .'

When he couldn't find a word that fit, Neil offered, 'A target. We focus on them, we show them what we want them to see. We hide from them, we hide from everyone else.'

Darren silently added, unless or until Mariana's secret contact reached out to them. He hoped it was someone with the clout to become a useful ally. But all he said was, 'Exactly.'

Leila inspected their chief scientist in her rearview mirror, then said, 'We might as well get this over with.'

Rising from the car proved to be a struggle. In the forty-eight-minute drive, Darren's body had become super-glued into position. Everything complained, even the components that had previously been silent. Even his toenails. Hair follicles.

Thankfully Anchali was there to support him over the endless trek from passenger seat to wheelchair. Neil showed him the plastic pouch holding the rainbow assortment of pain meds and anti-inflammatories. His other hand held a shopping bag full of prescriptions. 'You are two hours late for your next dose.'

Darren would have preferred to wait until he had gained a clear assessment of the opposition. But he was faced with a choice of being fogged by pain or drugs. 'Soon as we're inside.'

They crossed the sunbaked lot as a unit, everyone holding to the pace Neil set while pushing Darren's wheelchair. Together Leila and Anchali helped him rise and climb the three steps. Neil held the chair as he settled. As Leila held open the screen door, she offered him a look of genuine concern.

Friends.

An Air Force colonel was seated at the kitchen table drinking fresh-brewed coffee. The only thing this man had in common with Alveraz were the insignia on his lapels. Fernanda, their ever-silent chef, smiled a greeting and lifted the pot. Darren smiled, nodded, and allowed them to ease him into a chair at the table's head. He felt surprisingly good. He knew it was partly due to the plastic bag of meds Neil set beside his coffee. Mostly, though, it came down to how Darren now had a compass heading. The colonel's presence solidified their way forward. Darren's job was to help put the plan into action. As he swallowed the six pills followed by a slug of coffee, Darren was pretty certain he knew how. First step, anyway. Which was enough, for the moment.

Fernanda unwrapped the cellophane cover from a plate of cheese, fruit and antipasto. She set it on the table, then touched the forehead bordering Darren's bandage and spoke softly. Leila responded. Fernanda spoke again, and this time everyone replied except for Darren and the colonel.

The colonel said, 'I never could fit my head around the lingo. Tried and failed.'

'That puts you and me in the same boat,' Darren replied.

The officer reached across the table. 'Roger Abbott. I've been sent to take charge by the Pentagon.'

The final word was spoken like a military declaration. The Pentagon. A pronouncement from on high.

Wrong move, Darren thought.

Leila's laugh was a verbal punch. 'Take charge? You? Give me a break.'

'I have a master's in applied physics,' Abbott said.

This time Leila's laugh sounded almost genuine. 'From where, Iowa State?'

Abbott reddened. 'University of Kansas.'

'I can't believe they've sent us a *cretin* who has—'

'Leila,' Neil said.

'Who has the *audacity* to *think* for *one minute* that he could *possibly* comprehend what we're doing.'

'Enough,' Neil said. 'Please.'

Leila glared across the table. 'Not in a thousand years—'

'Please.' Anchali this time.

Her act of rising slammed the chair against the cabinets. Leila's ire was directed at everyone seated. 'Feel free to sit here and teach this Pentagon version of wasted space all the kindergarten physics he can handle. I'm off to do *real work.*'

The colonel was not portly in the sense of being fat, but he certainly was big. Every part of him was oversized, from the neck spilling over his collar to the fists planted on the table. Darren had a fleeting image of the Pentagon's structure bearing down on Abbott, pressing his bodily boundaries until he resembled the edifice – squat, heavy, ponderous, too large for his own good. It was impossible to be certain of his hair's shade, as it was cropped so short it blended into his pale scalp. If pressed, Darren would have guessed a blend of premature gray and blandest brown. He thought Abbott was aged around mid-forties, and wondered if the officer held any memories of ever being a child.

Anchali said quietly, 'I apologize on behalf of my colleague.'

Neil asked, 'I was told we answered to DARPA.'

Abbott kept his gaze on the empty screen door. 'And DARPA answers to the Pentagon.'

No one else spoke as Fernanda served a brunch of Spanish omelets and home fries. Darren waited for Neil to pour some soothing unguent on the colonel's singed ego. Instead, the silence held through the meal. As the meds gradually took hold, Darren sensed they were all waiting for him to take control. But the silence suited him. It helped define their way ahead. Effectively ignoring the red-faced officer who ate like an aging boxer, shoving in mouthfuls, grunting softly as he swallowed, all of this formed part of their next steps. Creating a clearly defined boundary. Us versus him and everyone he represented.

Anchali left first, carrying a plate for Leila. Then Neil. When it was just the two of them and the silent Fernanda, Abbott asked, 'Will somebody please tell me why the fellow signing the checks is suddenly the bad guy here?'

Darren used his shrug as a means of testing the drugs' reach. All seemed OK. He replied, 'Scientists.'

'I take it you're not one of that breed.'

'I'm an accountant, which you already know. Or should.'

Abbott looked down at his plate. Then, 'Will you tell me what's got the lady in a snit?'

'You should know that as well,' Darren replied. 'Yesterday's attack was the second this team has endured. The first was the week before last, when two professional assailants tried to take out Leila.'

'Sounds like the lady I'm replacing wasn't doing her job.'

Darren smiled, not at the colonel. Rather, at now having his own reason to dislike the guy. 'If you want to make allies of this team, you'll never mention anything like that ever again. Mariana was a friend to these people. They trusted her.'

The crimson flush creeped out of his collar, then receded. Abbott said, 'Noted.'

'Right now, they have no reason to think you're anything other than a representative of the enemy,' Darren said.

'That makes no sense. You know that, right? I mean, first DARPA tosses them a boatload of cash, then they come after this group? That defines idiocy.'

Darren hoped it wasn't just the drugs that made his responses so clearly laid out. He didn't think so. But he couldn't be sure. 'Let's pretend you're actually on our side. Which means your words are as idiotic as Leila suspects.'

Darren ignored the officer's flash of anger and continued, 'We both know the Pentagon holds multiple factions.' He pointed toward the lab. 'Our team suspects their opponents are minions doing the bidding of military suppliers. Corporations threatened by what this group might be able to achieve. These groups have two choices. Steal the data, or destroy the people responsible before they achieve the impossible.'

Darren stopped and waited. When he was certain the man was not going to respond, he went on, 'If you're on our side, prove it. Identify where the leak was, and who it went to.'

'My remit is to ensure it doesn't happen again.'

'It seems to me identifying the source is a good place to start,' Darren replied. 'That is, if you're really interested in getting on our good side.'

A silence, then, 'I'd expect a little gratitude for keeping you safe.'

'You know as well as I do, your version of safety could be just another way to keep this group caged.'

Abbott worked his jaw muscles. 'I'm not equipped with the resources to investigate what happened in the past.'

Darren saw no need to respond.

His silence only added to Abbott's ire. 'I'm not sure it's worth trying to get on anybody's good side. Especially that lady – what's her name?'

'Dr Leila Macias.'

'My remit doesn't say a thing about getting along with anybody. Being liked isn't a part of my duties unless I say so.'

Darren found himself liking how the colonel chewed off the ends of each word. Growling with irritation. Getting the man's fairly constant rage out in the open. Drawing clear lines in the sand. 'Let me take a short rest. Then why don't I show you around.'

The officer did not move. 'How come you're playing the good guy?'

'I've spent years working with the Pentagon.' Darren rose in cautious stages. 'It almost comes naturally.'

Abbott followed him into the library. 'So what's your duty around here?'

'Here's another suggestion,' Darren replied. 'Why don't you stop pretending you haven't spent hours studying our files.'

The colonel stood in the library doorway and watched as Darren eased down on to the sofa. Silent. Smoldering.

Darren stretched out, sighed with the simple pleasure of being prone. 'The question is are you really interested in being counted as a member of this team. Or is it enough to simply be tolerated.'

Abbott growled, 'How about I cut off the funding taps, see how long this hostility keeps running.'

Darren had met any number of such guys in his previous life. Military joes who were only comfortable with conflict. 'There are a number of preliminary steps you could take to become a welcome member. If you want.'

The silence lasted long enough for Darren to begin slipping away. Then, 'Such as?'

'Step one. Make sure there are no listening devices or cameras anywhere in the compound.' Darren was drifting away before his eyes were fully shut. He thought he managed to say, 'Ask someone to come wake me in an hour.'

Darren opened his eyes to find Leila seated beside the sofa. Watching him. Soon as he focused, she declared, 'Nothing was getting done in the lab. So I followed your lead. Went upstairs. Took a siesta. And I had one of those experiences. Your name fits. Dreamstate.'

He lifted a hand, gesturing for her to help him up. Soon as he was upright, he pointed to the pad and pen by the parlor's phone. She rose and brought it over, then stood over him as he wrote, *Do we have a way to detect a listening device or camera?*

She read, studied him briefly, then left the room.

Which was a shame, because Darren could have really used her help making it to the bathroom.

During what felt like a nearly endless trek, he discovered that while he slept someone had brought in a folding trundle bed. Two fruit-packing cases on the parlor table held his belongings. He selected boxers and shorts from the stack of clean clothes and entered the downstairs bath, where he discovered his shaving kit and bag of meds.

When he emerged, Leila pointed to a square metal box planted on the table next to his clothes. She pointed to a gleaming red light. 'We don't need to worry about monitoring equipment in the lab. First time we hit maximum power for a transit, we'd fry those devices.' She patted the box. 'When this is on, all outgoing signals are jammed. Don't use it in the kitchen; it messes with the microwave. And forget using a cellphone within a hundred feet.'

'Where's the colonel?'

'Gone. Left about an hour ago.'

Darren sorted through the stack of clean clothes, chose a shirt that buttoned up the front. 'Tell me about your dreamstate, please.'

She settled on the floor by the machine. 'If you hadn't described what you've been going through, I would have classed it as a weird moment brought on by the hospital. I haven't been in a medical clinic since my childhood.'

The side table held a single hard-back chair. Darren pulled it out, settled himself down. He felt every edge, every angle. But it would be easier to rise from this than the couch. 'So, this time you didn't experience another nightmare.'

'Not even close.' She tilted her chin, said to the ceiling, 'I went through some very hard days as a kid.'

Darren struggled to shove aside the drug's cushioning effects. 'Barry said something about that.'

She gave no sign she heard. 'They've left . . . stains. In this dreamstate, the stains, the memories . . .' She pushed a long breath through pursed lips. 'This isn't coming out right.'

'Leila, please, try.'

She looked at him. Really looked. 'You understand, don't you.'

'Since Gina's death, everything I see, touch, taste, breathe, experience. It's all been colored by what I went through.'

Her eyes were bottomless. 'Then you dreamed.'

'They're not dreams. But yes. When I entered that dreamstate, those burdens all vanished.'

She honored that with a moment's silence, then, 'Waking up afterward, it was awful.'

He nodded. 'Can you describe the event itself?'

'It didn't last long. Maybe a couple of minutes, probably less. I can't say; time really seemed to go away with everything else.'

'This as much as anything tells me we've experienced the same sort of moment. Time loses its hold.'

'I recognized it the very instant it started. And I was terrified I'd have another of those moments when the entity or whatever, or *whoever*, would want me dead.'

'But it was different.'

'Totally.'

'Did you have any impression of the . . . I don't know how to say this.' He searched, came up with, 'Did you get a sense, a flavor, of the experience?'

He knew he had expressed it poorly. Just the same, she nodded. 'Clinical. A very detached, very cold, very impersonal look at myself.'

Darren wondered if there was a risk in saying anything. Tainting her view, her memories, with his own. But she must have recognized his struggle for what it was. 'Go ahead. Say it.'

'There are four very distinct and very different entities in the unit I've been connected to.'

She studied him a long moment, the veil of hostility, the shields, the rigid emotional stance . . . Gone. 'You should name them.'

'I have. One was my first contact. I think of him as a liberal arts professor, distant, removed, aloof, extremely intelligent, but not at all focused. Two is . . . I don't know any other way to describe her except as the earth mother. Compassionate, wise, caring, healing. Full of grace and favor.'

'Wait. You've transited to more than one of the four?'

'I've only transited once, remember? And that link was with One, the professor. But apparently that transit-bond with the professor has left me open to *their* transits. All four. Inside these dreamstates.'

She rocked back. Forward. Back again. Absorbing the concept. 'What about the others?'

'Three. A lab geek. Not an original thinker. But vital.'

'And the last of the group?'

'Four is totally different. A force of nature. Incredibly intense. And so smart he's a little frightening.'

Another rock, then, 'Neil needs to hear this.'

'I agree.'

'This time he needs to pay attention.' She rose to her feet. 'Don't ask me to go back. Transit again. I can't risk what they did to me. What that other unit wanted to do.'

'Leila, it's not my place to ask you to do anything.'

But she wasn't done. 'Maybe if this dreamstate happens again. And if it's as nice as this time. Maybe then I'll go back. But after my final transit, it felt like I was targeted for death. That's what the dominant figure wanted. To have me dead, so I'd never come back there again.'

Leila monitored his progress down the hall, watched as he settled at the kitchen table, then departed. Darren made a mental note to start back on his morning exercises, testing joints, doing what came easy. Leila returned with his bag of prescriptions and announced, 'It's time for your next dose.'

'I'd rather wait.'

'And I'd rather be talking to Mariana than worrying about some parasite of a colonel watching over my shoulder.' She spoke to Fernanda, who brought him a glass of water. 'Every three hours. Doctor's orders.'

Darren opened the bag and began sorting out the next dose. He took one pill at a time, glancing at the scientist as he sipped from his mug. Now that her guard was at least partly down, Leila was heart-stoppingly beautiful.

Fernanda brought him a steaming mug, then spoke to Leila, who said, 'You recently lost your wife?'

'I told you that.'

'The way you said it, I thought it was years back.'

He shook his head. 'Gina passed away seven months ago.'

Leila addressed Fernanda while still watching him, then, 'Fernanda asks if your appearance of holding up well from the burden of loss is the truth.'

He liked the formal translation, as if Leila was too caught up in what she heard to shift Fernanda's question fully into English. He also liked the way Fernanda watched him, her gaze as caring and gentle as her voice. Not to mention the spark of something new in how Leila studied him. Both women revealed shadows and intelligence in equal measure. 'It's very good to have a reason to look beyond the loss.'

Then Fernanda said something more, and Leila offered them both a rare smile. '*Pendiente.* Oh, wow.'

'What's that?'

'Fernanda's made dulce de leche cake,' Leila replied, still smiling. 'Think of the absolute best caramel dessert you've ever had, then amp it by a factor of twenty.'

'You should smile more often,' Darren said. He watched as Fernanda cut him a slice and set an old-timey blue porcelain plate in front of him. His portion was huge. 'I hope she's going to help me eat this.'

Leila smiled again as Fernanda served her. 'Wait until you try it. Then we'll see who has too much on his plate.'

The cake was an astonishment, the caramel filling treacly smooth and so rich his teeth hurt. 'OK, this is . . .'

'I know, right?'

The cake seemed to vanish of its own accord. Once his plate was empty and he had scraped out the last tiny bit of caramel, he said, 'I have an idea. I figure if I can convince you, I'll be more than halfway to everybody else being on my side.'

'That actually makes sense.' Another exchange, then, 'Fernanda asks if you want more.'

'Absolutely. Just not now. Please tell her that is the finest dessert I've ever tasted.'

Leila swept her fork over the empty plate as she spoke a soft melody to the smiling chef, then asked him, 'Am I wrong to like you?'

'Leila . . . I only want what is good for you and the team.'

She remained unmoved. Silent. Very still.

He could feel the meds gradually take hold, and knew there was only a brief window before his clarity became dulled. 'I need to ask about your contacts on the transit's other side.'

'Just the one contact for each of us.'

'Always the same individual for each of you, right?'

She nodded. 'Neil thinks it's tied to the singularity that defines second sound.'

'OK. And there was one individual who was opposed to the others shutting you out, did I get that right?'

'Neil's contact.'

'How did the others react?'

'My contact protested. But mildly. Anchali says it felt like her contact broke ranks and tried to reach out to us anyway. Neil's contact was furious. After that our two contacts did what the other one said. Like they were obeying.' She was fully absorbed now, unblinking. 'I never thought of this before, how it relates to what you said about your group flowing together. Anchali and my transit partners, the pair who wanted to help us – it absolutely infuriated this leader. But they made no move against him.' Another pause. 'Where are you going with this?'

'The impression I had of my four was the exact opposite of what you're describing. Except for the one who was totally in charge. I got that too.'

Leila nodded. 'You said they liked having you there.'

'It was more than that. The instant I transited, they melded together, or joined, whatever.' He waited to see if she understood. 'Leila, it's not like they just welcomed me. They made me part of their unit. All four wanted to unite with me. So what if this means I can ask their help with the missing elements to your equations?'

Leila studied him a long moment. 'There's a serious problem with your idea. You're not a physicist. We have no idea if they are either.'

'I've thought of that.' He described his idea in as few words as possible. He finished with, 'Time is not our friend. There's only one way of knowing. And our window . . .'

Her eyes widened. 'You want to make this happen *right now*?'

'It needs to happen while our new watcher is away. So yes.'

Leila was already on her feet. 'You just come with me.'

'The first time we succeeded in making a transit was a total fluke,' Neil said. 'Right up there with Newton's apple.'

Darren sat on the plastic stool and tried to remain still while Neil fit on the headset. Through the cage's front wall he could see Leila hammering her keyboard. His momentary glimpse of a sweeter, happier lady was history.

Upon entering the lab, Leila told them Darren's big idea. Skipped the windup, went straight for the main event. Darren couldn't tell if Neil's excited response was because he thought the idea might actually work, or if it simply gave them a concrete reason to risk another transit. Despite Darren's weakened and wounded state.

Once seated in the glass transit cage, Darren again described his take on these sleep-time experiences being more than dreams. Neil listened, mostly because Leila ordered him to. All while, though, Neil prepped. Darren could tell from the outset that Neil still considered it a sidebar issue. Which totally infuriated Leila, and explained her current attempt to hammer the keyboard into submission.

Darren's meds blanketed him in a layer of medical calm. He told Neil, 'You really need to pay more careful attention to these dreamstates.'

Neil followed Darren's gaze over to where Leila fumed. 'Leila, can you hear me?'

When the younger scientist refused to respond, Anchali said, 'Loud and clear.'

'Say you're both right. You're describing a new dimension to the entire transit event horizon. We have uncovered a means by which aliens are using *our* sleep-states as opportunities to enter *our* world and bond.'

Leila's hands slowed, stilled. She looked up. Angry. But listening.

'I didn't handle it well. I apologize.' Neil pointed to Darren seated on the stool. 'But Darren's idea of trying to enlist his unit in unraveling these equations is a good one. Right now, the colonel is off doing military things. Like Darren said, we have this immediate time window to determine if there is actually something—'

'All right, all right.' Leila waved one hand over her head. 'You've made your point. Can we get started?'

Neil grinned at Darren and went back to adjusting the headgear. 'You OK there, sport?'

'Those little digits poke my skull. Don't press so hard.'

'Sorry.' He spoke louder, 'Anchali, how are the readouts?'

'All good.'

'Leila?'

'Alignment is five by five.'

'I love it when things go right.' He plugged the headgear's fiber-optic lead into the floor socket. 'What was I talking about?'

'The first transit was a total fluke.'

Neil looked at him. Serious. A rare still moment for Darren's friend, the brilliant geeky teen who grew into a totally geeky adult. 'Thanks, man. You know. For doing this.'

He waved that aside. 'You were talking about the fluke of a first transit.'

'I was in the cage,' Neil told him. 'Waiting for Leila to stop fiddling with her controls.'

'Correction. I was trying to align the power amps,' Leila said, her voice coming through the floor speakers, sounding surprisingly calm. 'Which our boss scientist guy had insisted on messing with. For hours beyond count.'

But Neil was smiling as he backed away from the chamber. 'It's amazing how heavy that rubber mallet can get, climbing the ladder, whacking at those things, climbing down, shifting to the next, whacking again. I was standing where the stool is now, and told Leila to go for maximum amp and check the calibrations.'

Leila announced, 'Thirty seconds to full power.'

'So there I was,' Neil said, pulling the whiteboard in so close to the cage's front wall all Darren could see was the maze of symbols. The unfinished formula. 'One second I was waiting for Leila to tell me which gizmo needed another whack. The next, and I was back from talking with the fairies.'

Leila said, 'Ten seconds.'

Neil sealed him in.

Darren took a long last look at the whiteboard. His plan seemed so feeble now. Show these members of an unknown species an equation using symbols that were absolutely not their own. Communicated by a guy who didn't have a clue what it all meant, and would probably forget the most important elements. Crazy.

The whiteboard's empty spaces and unresolved mysteries were marked by question marks. Which meant absolutely nothing to anyone who didn't use their alphabet. Or to Darren, for that matter.

Crazy.

Just the same, he felt a genuine sense of very real hope. Clearly there was a meshing of minds involved. And if this had happened with the other group, and Darren's four contacts dwelling on their planet's surface in the forbidden zone connected at the same mental level, and if at least some of them were physicists, why couldn't they figure out what the symbols represented and provide the missing ones?

A lot of ifs.

Just the same, no one else had a better idea.

And the clock was ticking.

Leila said, 'Three, two, one . . .'

FOURTEEN

S*NAP.*

FIFTEEN

In his first instant of returning consciousness, Darren became entombed.

An external force gripped him so tightly he could scarcely breathe. As if some shadowy component of the transit had returned with him, an entity so potent it threatened to stifle, crush, suffocate . . .

It was gone.

Darren opened his eyes. They were all there, gathered around him, watching, worried. He realized they had already transferred him to the gurney. He felt the electrodes hooking him to the machines that blinked and beeped. The oxygen mask was in place, filling his lungs. He relished the sensation of blood coursing through his body, filling him with the exquisite assurance of life.

Neil asked if he was all right. Darren felt his friend's concerns. He did not hear words. Instead, there was a recognition at some deeper level that his friend had spoken. He could not respond just yet. A nod was beyond him. The otherworldly seizure was gone. The fear remained. Every breath was a defiance. A gift.

They thought he was still recovering. This was true and not true. The transit unraveled behind his eyes. Neil had been right about that element. Time did not count the same during the transit. For the first time, Darren saw it in sequence.

He waited until he was able to fathom the individual train of events. Then Darren lifted a hand, and the others took it as a sign he was ready to sit up. He pulled off the oxygen mask and swiveled so that his feet dangled over the gurney's side. He needed to tell them what had happened. But something else was more important. He was filled with a vital need, strong as the desire to draw his next breath.

Darren rose, grateful for the meds' cushioning effect. Hands took hold of his arms, another rested on his back. Voices protested, questioned his movements. He was aware, but unable to speak. With their help, he made it to the first empty whiteboard. He did not glance at the one still resting in front of the cage, all the work it represented. He picked up a felt pen, fumbled with the cap, then reached up and began writing.

He made swift notations and filled the whiteboard in less than three minutes. Even before he reached the bottom-right corner, Leila had rolled over the next. They exclaimed, demanded, asked him this and that. Their voices were a gentle goad, a chorus of concern, gradually drawing him back.

He reached a stopping point, a pause in the torrent. The moment carried an electric surge, almost like he underwent a mini-*SNAP*. His entire body shook from the force of reliving what he had experienced during the transit. The recollection could not be described as seeing, for while there were visual images attached, they were limited. Brief glimpses of the terrain, the two suns, a moon, some odd four-winged birds, a cone-shaped city drifting like a green-gold cloud. He had no idea what his contacts looked like. He suspected this was intentional, keeping a tight focus, allowing him to see nothing that might totally bug him out.

Neil stepped up beside him and asked, 'Is that it?'

'No.' The memory was so intense the whiteboard became a frame for what he now saw. 'Are you recording?'

Anchali rushed away, called, 'Rolling.'

The pressure to speak, to reveal what he had seen and get back to the written work, was so intense his entire body trembled. He knew his voice shook, but he was fairly certain the words remained clear enough.

'You were right, thinking the transit lasts longer than what we experience at this end. How long, I have no idea. The feeling was more like, time holds a different definition over there.'

He spoke so fast the words jumbled. He was desperately afraid the clarity would fade. Plus there was more to the equation that he needed to get down. 'They were hoping we would try this or something like it. Soon as I showed up, my contact joined with the others.'

'The professor,' Leila offered. 'One. That's who you mean?'

'Yes.' The bond within her words, the power of being

understood, threatened his connection to the other side. 'Best if you don't speak.'

'Sorry.'

'They joined,' he repeated. 'And I joined with them. This made the transfer of what's there on your board a totality. No, that's the wrong way to describe what happened.'

'We understand,' Neil said. 'Go on.'

'The one I call Four, the chief scientist, took over. There was a super-fast conversation with the second scientist, the lab geek – but it wasn't enough. They were having a lot of trouble with the translation, understanding what some things meant, and so they decided to link again. One, the professor, needed to be part of it. He understands more of our interpretation of life. The link needed to be total so they could work inside our mathematical language . . .'

The realization of what happened next sent tremors strong as convulsions through his frame. He was grateful for the meds. They muted the experience enough for him to actually speak. 'Something alerted them to the enemy. The ones hunting them. My awareness became split in two. The professor and two scientists remained caught up in completing this formula. It's what you thought. A means of harnessing dark energy. And something more. The energy has to be refashioned so it translates to our three-dimensional existence. Dark energy is not held by the same structure. But it's also fluid, open to reinterpretation.'

Neil murmured, 'Are you hearing this?'

Leila hissed. Then, 'Go on, Darren. Your awareness was divided.'

The convulsions trapped him. A mere shadow of what he had known in that dark, tight instant of dread. When he could speak, he said, 'The earth mother, that's my term for the second contact. The feminine aspect of this four. She broke free. But the separation wasn't total. She fled, and in that instant of departure they remained at least partly joined. She carried part of my awareness with her. She flew up and entered the floating city. She gave the hunters a target. And she kept them from realizing the others were down on their planet. I had my first true glimpse of their civilization. And it almost killed me.' A trio of gasping breaths.

Fist to his gut, pushing back against the nausea. Then, 'She's gone.'

Leila was the one who framed the question, her voice a nearly broken cry. 'What do you mean, gone?'

'They trapped her.' The memory of that instant's clenching force was merely a shadow of what Darren had experienced. Even so, it was enough to leave him gasping for breath. 'The city-state's hunters stifled her. They crushed out her life. She used her last moment to push me away. And the others. It was her final act of defiance. Keeping us alive.'

Soon as he stopped talking, the tremors halted and the equation solidified once more.

Darren returned to the whiteboard and wrote. The only sound in that vast chamber was the soft whine of his pen on the surface.

When he was done, the impact was shattering. He did not step back. Darren slumped so hard and so fast his forehead struck the whiteboard's protruding metal rack. But he felt nothing, since he was already gone.

Darren had no idea how long he was under before the dreamstate began. He welcomed the release, though it was no longer truly an escape. Rather, he entered into a different existence, one with its own jagged edges.

The three who remained now had a loss of their own. An absence that tore apart their unified whole.

If only they could mourn.

In this dreamscape, he was joined by the secondary scientist, the lab geek. Darren observed the same sort of request or invitation, both fit and neither were right. He acquiesced and moved with Three, as Darren thought of him. Rising more easily this time from his physical awareness. There was no need to protest, or anything to be afraid of. The scientist offered him a somber affirmation. The two of them were in this together now.

Three did a slow sweep of the entire lab, before focusing intently on the whiteboard holding their initial calculations. From there they shifted over to the two boards now holding his own work – the new calculations shared by Four. The dreamstate awareness returned to the first one, back and forth, analyzing and delving and seeing what else was required. Darren sensed a harmony, a distinct approval and satisfaction. They were on target. No question about it. But there was still much to be done.

He and his dreamstate companion watched as Neil worked on yet another whiteboard, Leila and Anchali on one of the easels stationed alongside him. The three of them talked and wrote in simultaneous haste. Breaking down what Darren had brought back. He and his alien visitor observed in disembodied approval.

Then Darren became captured by a realization of his own, the thought so powerful he became the one who pulled back and drew in. A first.

He lay on the gurney, aware of his body, and drifted.

This in-between state was new. No longer connected to the alien, and yet not totally bound by his own human definition of life and awareness. This disconnect granted him a new position from which he could study these new transitions.

The dreamstate's freedom from emotional burdens and hard-edge memories, the sense of utter liberation, the intense focus on *now*: everything Darren found so remarkable about his dreamstates were precisely what defined this alien group.

The loss of Two, the earth mother who had sacrificed herself in order to mask the others' location, this absence also contained another monumental element. Her departure robbed the other three of their ability to feel anything at all.

Regret, sorrow, the burdens of past and future – all gone. Leaving the trio with one shred of purpose to their rebellion in the time they had left. A final act of mathematical defiance.

Darren felt a genuine pressure to share this urgency with the rest of the team. Because the longer he lay there, the more certain he became that they were not even close to getting it all. This wasn't just about harnessing dark energy. Four was sharing more than that . . . This time shared in front of the whiteboards with his alien visitor carried both approval and need, as in, there was a great deal more they had to access. And time was against them. However time was measured in the world of floating cities, it was running out.

* * *

But when Darren rose slowly from the gurney, he realized any message about unfinished equations and the aliens' urgent need to continue had to wait. He remained partially hidden behind the movable hospital screens. Which was good, because Abbott was back and inside the lab.

Darren actually didn't mind hitting the pause button. His wheelchair was stationed by the side wall, and he was too whacked out to care where he rested. Darren settled in the chair and positioned himself where he could observe the three scientists standing around the central whiteboard. Leila was making notes on an easel lined up alongside, while Anchali and Neil argued over some component of Darren's message.

The burly colonel leaned against the far wall, frowning. Abbott clearly disliked being ignored. Darren watched as Abbott strode across the room, moving like an irritated bull. Determined to insert himself into the discussion. 'Looks to me like you might have a breakthrough.'

For once, Leila held herself in check.

Neil did not even turn from the board. 'Maybe. Just maybe.'

'The first glint of light at the end of the tunnel,' Anchali agreed.

Abbott visibly perked up. Surprised at their willingness to include him. 'Can you tell me what's happening?'

Neil glanced at the ladies standing on either side. 'It may be good to develop a progress report.'

'OK,' Leila said, her voice unnaturally soft.

'Give us another hour,' Neil said.

'Two,' Leila said, pointing at some empty space on the third whiteboard. 'Two hours.'

'Then we'll meet in the parlor—'

'Kitchen,' Anchali said. 'Darren is using the parlor as his temporary bedroom.'

'Oh. Right. Kitchen it is.'

'Good. OK. Primo.' Abbott started away, then, 'Oh. One thing. I've arranged for a security specialist to scan the entire compound for bugs. He's due any minute.'

Leila said, 'Not here. Not now.'

'Start in the house,' Anchali said. 'He can scan here while we meet in the kitchen.'

'OK. Primo. Well, I'll just . . .'

When they were alone, Leila asked, 'How did I do?'

'Primo,' Anchali said.

Darren pushed the chair forward and into view, and told Leila, 'I think a standing ovation is in order.'

As Neil started over, Anchali said, 'Only if she can manage the sweetness and light routine for the rest of the day do we applaud.'

'Don't ask the impossible,' Leila replied.

Neil took control of the wheelchair. 'Where are we headed?'

'Bathroom.'

As Neil helped him transit the lab, aiming for the bathroom at the chamber's far end, Leila started over. 'You're past due for your meds.'

His body offered all the confirmation Darren required. He took more pills from the plastic bag, accepted the water bottle, swallowed. 'Thank you, Leila.'

Anchali said, 'See what happens when you play nice?'

Leila flashed him a smile, replied, 'Really not worth it.'

Darren rose from the chair and entered the bathroom on his own steam. His body still ached in all the wrong places. There was also leakage through the bandage on his forehead. Just the same, he was fairly certain he had rounded yet another corner.

Darren walked mostly unassisted on the return journey, testing his balance and his strength. Neil kept one hand hovering just off his shoulder, nothing more. Soon as he had their attention he said, 'I need to go back.'

Clearly they all assumed he meant returning to the farmhouse. Settle into the parlor. Bathe and eat and have a deeper rest.

So he added, 'Transit.'

Their response was almost comic. Three identical expressions. African American, Thai, Latina. Shocked and horrified both.

Neil said, 'You can't be serious.'

Darren had neither the interest nor the energy to argue. So he started shuffling toward the glass cage. 'Soon as I'm seated, you need to start recording. I'll explain while you prep.'

They all said it together. 'But Darren. No . . .'

'We need to do this while Abbott is busy with the security joe.'

The fact that Darren was already inside the cage, settling

on the stool, intent and ready, finally mobilized them. 'I need to give you something more from the last transit while you set up.'

Leila was already seated at her console, flipping switches, making adjustments. She said, 'Rolling.'

Darren described in greater detail the earth mother's ultimate sacrifice. How he was joined enough to feel her capture, yet sufficiently distant to survive. He shifted from there to his most recent dreamstate.

He could almost script the moment when Neil's impatience got the better of him. Neil snapped, 'Now isn't the time.'

'Sorry, but you're wrong.'

'Darren, we're prepping you for another transit despite all the reasons to take a giant step back and give you a chance to fully recover.'

'And I'm telling you these dreamstates play a crucial role.' He felt the new dosage of meds gradually plucking away any energy he might otherwise have used to press home the point. 'These dreamstates can't wait.'

Neil helped him set the plastic headgear in place. 'I'm still not clear on why yet another transit is so crucial we risk genuinely impacting your long-term health.'

Leila rose from her chair. Started over. Something in the way she carried herself, the set of her jaw, the coal-dark burn in her gaze, silenced Neil.

She stepped into the cage's doorway. Spoke with a viper's calm. 'You will be silent. And you will listen.'

Darren found it easier to watch her while he said, 'The union or whatever you want to call it, this joining that takes place in the dreamstates, it's growing stronger. Twice now, first in the hospital and when I zonked out after scribbling on the whiteboard, I've gone walkabout.' He gave that a moment, then added, 'I'm talking, inside the dreamstate.'

Leila's ire vanished in a flash of understanding. 'You and the alien. Together.'

'Right. I saw Neil and Anchali working on the whiteboard while you wrote on the easel.' He watched as Anchali rose and joined Leila in the doorway. 'The alien studied what I had scripted from the last transit, and then gave a careful inspection to what you were working on. There was this total sense of confirmation. You're on the right track with dark energy and the seemingly non-related new equations I received after reaching out to my unit for their help to complete the formula. But it was also clear that we're a long way from getting it all done.'

'I don't . . .' Neil pointed to the array of whiteboards and easels. 'It's right there in front of us.'

'If he says it's not, you need to listen,' Leila said.

Anchali was almost gentle, like she was addressing a child. 'Darren, what we have for dark energy seems enough. We just need to understand it.'

'It is enough in a way. But it's only chapter one. There's more. That's what the new calculations represent, although what that is, I don't yet know.' He looked from one to the other. 'The message is as totally clear as anything I've had since this started. We're miles from getting it all. And they don't have much time. Sooner or later this enemy is going to realize the remaining three are hiding out in the forbidden zone. And our chance at getting the rest will be lost.' Darren pulled the hated headgear down tight over his scalp and said, 'Let's get this started.'

SIXTEEN

S*NAP.*

SEVENTEEN

There was no time for rest, though his body craved it like a starving man did food. They tried to stop him, keep him there on the gurney. Anchali even said something about his heart's irregular beat. Nothing mattered except the need to rise and walk to the empty whiteboard and write.

Darren filled the space with symbols and graphs that meant nothing, except for the critically urgent need to expel. Write. Get it down. Move on.

During brief rests Darren described how he connected as always with the individual in the unit he thought of as One, with the distant air of a professor. One had instantly handed him off, the act made possible through an incomplete joining. There was no better way to describe the three of them coming together, unable to emotionally access the wound of their absent mate.

Darren was then bounced back and forth between the two physicists, the leader's elephantine force and the lab assistant's calmer mode of interpreting. Filling in the blanks left by the leader's frantic push toward a conclusion very far out ahead of them.

There was more to be said, but Darren stopped talking because his energy was draining away, the act of forming words taking too much from what still needed to be put down. He wrote until his hand cramped, the fingers so tight he couldn't keep hold of the pen. Anchali stepped in, applying pressure to various points, while Leila drew over another whiteboard and held out a fresh pen. Darren took it and wrote. And wrote. And wrote. Then suddenly he was done, and the waves of fatigue were simply overwhelming. All he could manage to say was a single word, a desperate plea. Food.

They settled him in the wheelchair and hustled him back across the rear yard, rushing past Abbott and some stranger, Darren assumed it was the technician. The colonel demanded to know what had happened, and Leila of all people stopped and spun some fable of Darren working on the necessary forms until he almost collapsed. Abbott responded with the expected command for Darren to take it easy, the forms would still be there the next day. By which point Neil and Anchali were already helping him up the rear stairs and into the kitchen.

Darren ate like some ravenous half-tamed beast of the wild, tasting nothing, devouring whatever was there in front of him, pressed to frantic haste by the certainty he was going down hard.

So hard, in fact, that for the first time since his initial transit, Darren did not actually welcome the dreamstate's arrival. The novelty, the freedom, the thrill were all there. Yet this time when the professor he'd named One arrived, Darren remained distinctly separate. One was made uncertain by Darren's response. The alien clearly expected Darren to be trusting, compliant. But he had lost Two, the feminine aspect of their unit. And now this. So One remained at a somewhat distracted distance. He fumed for a time in a distinctly alien and non-emotional manner. Then he left.

When sleep finally released him, Darren made his fumbling way to the bathroom. He returned and settled, then rose again and took his night-time meds. When he slipped back into his trundle bed and waited for sleep to return, he found himself viewing his burdens from a totally different perspective.

For the first time ever, he searched beyond the dreamscape's gift of release. Seeing instead what such an existence might truly mean. A life where there was no feeling at all.

These four had joined illegally. What had life been for them before taking that forbidden step? What was life now that they had lost their emotional link? Were they even capable of missing the one who had felt for them all? Were they aware of what they now lacked?

And what about himself? He had come to dread those moments following the dreamscape's release. Yet would he be willing to forgo all emotions, if life lost its ability to wound him anew?

Even asking the question filled him with an acidic bile. Only some philosopher locked inside a safe ivory-town existence would bother with such idiocy. His life had not come with an opt-out clause. He had loved, he had lost, and now he paid the price of giving himself fully to another. End of discussion.

The internal debate exhausted him. He fell into the dark ashes of all that was no more, and slept.

EIGHTEEN

Darren woke eleven hours later. He took his time, unkinking muscles and tendons as he moved to the bathroom. He was beyond late taking his next dose of meds, and his muscles complained at full volume. Just the same, he held off. He went through a shadow-boxing parody of his morning routine. Doing a slight trace of each exercise, not coming close to pushing his aching body. He wanted to do this while his mind was free of the meds, so he could tell when to back off.

He took the meds and showered a very long time, the water hot enough to scald. As he dressed, an idea began to take hold. Darren had the distinct impression it had been forming all night. Only now in the midday light was he able to see the new compass heading. He walked slowly down the corridor, taking the time necessary to shape his next steps.

Fernanda greeted him and poured a fresh mug without being asked. Then she pointed in the lab's direction and spoke words he didn't need to understand. She pushed through the rear screen door and hustled across the rear yard, leaving him to sit and enjoy his coffee. When she returned, Leila was with her, Fernanda chatting softly as they climbed the steps and crossed the porch. Leila entered and asked, 'How are you?'

'Good. Better than that.' He held his mug out for Fernanda to refill. 'How are things at ground zero?'

She spoke swiftly with their chef, then replied, 'Good. Better than that.'

'Was that a joke?'

'I never joke.'

'I don't know, Leila, I thought maybe I heard a small joke there.'

She tasted a smile, one that almost captured her eyes. Then, 'Anchali is worried about a possible irregularity in your heart rate after that last transit. She insists you wait another day before you go again. Neil agrees. And Barry.' When Darren started to argue, she held up her hand. 'If you want to object, take it to the lab. But I'm telling you straight up, it won't do any good.'

He remained silent and watched Fernanda prepare what he was fairly certain would soon be a Mexican-style omelet. 'Where's the colonel?'

'In your office with Barry. Talking forms and money.' She tapped three fingers on the table, counting out her softly spoken words. 'Last night I had another dreamstate. So did Anchali. Very quick, but also very nice.'

'Both of you?'

She nodded. 'We had the impression it was a different situation. The flavor was not the same as before. Do you know what I mean?'

Something about the news left his gut crawling with electric worms. 'Not really.'

'Before, soon as the nightmare started, I knew it was the one I connected with during transit. I know flavor doesn't suit but I can't come up with anything better.'

'Flavor works fine.'

'Anchali is certain her flavor was different this time too. Much more definite than me. I had this hint, nothing more. Only after she told me did I think that maybe she was expressing what I had felt. Again, we're talking about an experience that flashed into existence for three or four breaths. Not longer.' When he did not respond, she looked up. 'What do you think that means?'

'I'm not sure.'

'Anchali said something else.' Leila watched him now, her gaze a dark well. 'She thinks your four have reached out and they want us to transit.'

He corrected, 'It's three now.'

Leila nodded. 'If Anchali is right, it means our having made a transit to the other group now opens us to contacts beyond the initial connection.'

Darren did not know what to say, so he remained silent.

'I find a distinct harmony in thinking it's your group who have reached out. And did so only long enough to offer, I don't know how to say this.'

'A sort of welcome?' Darren suggested. 'Or invitation?'

'Yes. That definitely works.'

'So what happens now?'

'Anchali tried to discuss this with Neil. It's hard to say if he even heard what she was trying to tell him. His attention is totally zeroed in on the work at hand.' Leila shifted around so as to stare out the rear door. 'I don't care what Anchali thinks, I just don't feel able to take that step.'

'What step are we talking about?'

'Doing a transit, seeing if the invitation is real and coming from your team.' Leila turned to him, her expression worried. 'Anchali thinks she should go. Time is short, and connecting with a trained physicist at this end could speed things up.' Another pause, then, 'Neil isn't saying, but my guess is we're getting so much from your transits he doesn't want to take that risk.'

There was no reason the news would leave him so unsettled. Everything Leila reported made perfect sense. He decided it was best to stay quiet until he had a clearer handle on what was behind his concerns.

When he did not respond, Leila rose from the table. 'I better get back, make sure Neil puts all the ones and zeros in the right places.'

'Another joke.'

'I told you. I don't joke.'

'Leila, wait.' When she turned around, he decided it was time to put his plan in motion. 'I'm thinking it would be good to get away for the day. Maybe spend a few hours at the shore. Have some time to myself after everything that's been happening.' He gave that a beat, then added as casually as he could, 'Take the colonel off your hands.'

'For that I'd pay good money.' She pointed in the lab's direction. 'Once the security consultant finished checking for bugs, Abbott kept trying to insert himself in our calculations. As if the man could come up with one decent idea. Barry dragged him into your office when we started having homicidal thoughts.'

He smiled his thanks as Fernanda set a plate in front of him. He debated asking Barry to accompany them, then decided if the plan should include his old friend it would have been set in place long before now. 'Ask the colonel if he'd mind taking a ride.'

Darren pointed through the sun-dappled windscreen. 'That's your turn up ahead on your right.'

The colonel slowed and glanced over, his expression doubtful. 'You're sure this is it?'

'I was only here once. But yeah, I'm . . . Left fork.' A half-mile later, he said, 'Might be a good idea to honk your horn.' When Abbott shot him another look, Darren explained, 'Be the polite thing to do, since they don't know your car.'

Abbott gave it three beeps, then, 'Why are you doing this?'

'You did what we asked. Brought in the security consultant to check for bugs. This is me saying thanks.'

All three stood outside the central tent. Worried. Tense. Darren remembered the woman's name was Mora. There was no question which of the three was Tank. The third . . .

Mora walked over, studied them through Darren's open window, offered him a fist.

Darren gave it the requested bump, hoping he got that right. Mora told the others, 'This is the guy I told you about.'

'Darren,' he offered.

'He came with Mariana that last time.' To Darren, 'How is our lady?'

'I assume you've spoken with Tanaka, which means you know what I know. She's still in the induced coma, but her vitals remain stable.' Darren indicated the car's driver. 'This is Roger Abbott.'

Mora did not even glance over. 'Tanaka said something about the docs maybe waking our pal up.'

'Right. Tomorrow. If her swelling keeps reducing.'

Still not even a look in Abbott's direction. 'Why are you here?'

'Neil thought it would be a good way to say thanks to our new temp, showing him your camp.'

Abbott spoke for the first time. 'Don't call me that.' When neither of them looked his way, he continued, 'I'm on duty for the duration. My remit is open-ended.'

Mora continued to hold Darren's eye. He asked, 'You need anything?'

'Tanaka's due in an hour or so. We're good. But thanks.' Mora straightened, nodded a farewell. 'If you see the lady, tell her we're hanging tight. Like she'd want.'

They did not speak again during the drive south. Forty-five minutes later, Abbott pulled into a space flanking the Melbourne Beach boardwalk. Darren thought it was the same spot where he had been chained to the railing, all those many eons ago, but he couldn't be certain.

Abbott asked, 'You sure you'll be OK?'

Darren opened his door. 'I need this.'

Abbott watched him rise in stages, working out the kinks. 'You still look all banged up.'

'I'll be fine.'

'Darren, wait.' When he leaned back down, Abbott said, 'My remit is to keep you folks safe. It doesn't say anything about giving somebody the afternoon to wander around on their lonesome.'

Darren had the distinct impression Abbott was mentally already back on the road, heading off to do whatever. The man was just ticking the boxes on his military form. 'You know as well as I do, I'm the fifth wheel. The people you need to worry about are all back in the lab.'

Abbott nodded agreement. 'You want, I could pick you up later.'

Darren closed the door, pretended to give the offer serious consideration, then leaned down and said through the open window, 'Appreciate the offer. But I want to walk as far as I can, maybe grab a bite somewhere. I'll call for an Uber when I'm ready.'

'Cost you a fortune.'

Darren smiled at that. 'DARPA is already spending a fortune. This will get lost in the wash.'

Abbott did not protest further. Instead, he asked, 'If you were in my position, what would you check on next? Getting firmly tucked into the work and people.'

The question caught Darren off guard. 'You know about Tanaka's project?'

'Karate center, right?'

'It's a lot more than that. Titusville is on your way back. You should stop by, have a word with his wife. Orna is as much a part of this as anyone.' When Abbott looked doubtful, he added, 'Your stopping by will mean a lot to the whole team. And something else: Tanaka knows more than anyone about that first attack on Leila. He trained her. Apparently that's why she survived.'

Abbott offered him a grudging thanks, put the car in gear, then was halted by Darren saying, 'One thing more.'

'Shoot.'

'We both know you've got people investigating the incident. Trying to determine who was behind the attack.'

The colonel shook his head. 'Not my remit. The US military is the world's finest at compartmentalizing.'

'Just the same—'

'Like I said before, don't ask for what I can't give. And I don't know about any leak.'

Abbott waited until Darren was well clear of the car, then backed from the space and drove away.

Darren took his time climbing the boardwalk's four steps, keeping a firm grip on the handrail and pausing at the top. Then he proceeded slowly south. Away from the beachside shops and the worst of the tourist crowds.

Ten careful steps further along, a woman's voice said, 'That was a smart move, making this journey just another part of the colonel's day.'

NINETEEN

The woman was as finely drawn as a kabuki mask. Everything about her was meaningless. At least, all that Darren could see. She was dressed in a city woman's version of beachside fashion: pastel slacks and floral blouse and matching sandals. She was aged somewhere in her mid-to-late fifties, graying hair precisely trimmed, much of her face hidden behind oversized glasses. The crowds thinned as they continued south, which brought the woman's security detail into clearer focus. She was shadowed by two individuals, one male and one female, drifting along their periphery. Looking everywhere except at the woman they shielded.

When it was just the two of them and her security, Darren asked, 'Do I want to know who you are?'

'Want, I can't say. Need, that's for later.' She pointed to an empty bench, then waited as Darren eased himself down. 'I'm here so you can fill me in on what's happened since you were attacked. Plus, I thought it was time to obtain a personal assessment. Determine whether you are someone who deserves DARPA's confidence.' She watched him settle. 'If things go smoothly, you may never see me again.'

'But you'll be there.'

'Whenever, wherever.' She seated herself next to Darren, then reached into a blue lizard shoulder-bag and passed him a sleek black phone. 'Next-gen satellite device. My number is taped to the back. Memorize it and destroy the paper.'

'It's heavy.'

'Compared to older models, it's nothing.' She pointed to the blank screen. 'Once I answer, press the skull and crossbones app for automatic encryption.'

'Cute.'

'My in-house security geeks have a twisted sense of humor.' She watched him pocket the phone. 'Tell me what's happened since Colonel Abbott joined your team.'

Darren hesitated. 'Can I ask how much you know?'

She showed no irritation to his request. No emotions whatsoever. 'Transits are as good a name as any for what brings you into contact with an alien race. I know you're their only functioning conduit since Neil and the others were shut out.'

'So, you basically know everything.' And he knew how. This was Mariana's contact.

'My access to Neil's recordings and project summaries ended with the attack,' she replied. 'We had Mariana's hospital room bugged, so I know you had a plan for continuing the team's work. I assume these plans included your going back in.'

'I've transited back twice more.'

She nodded, then spoke more softly, 'Report.'

Darren started by explaining his vague plan, surveying unfinished calculations that were mere whiteboard scribblings to him. He described how the transits had been enormously successful in bringing back additional components to these new calculations. As he described his desperate need to write it all down, his hand began cramping once more.

Darren continued with the next transit, and upon his return the desperate need to proceed. Accelerate. Reveal faster. He described writing on the whiteboards and the easels, not caring that he did not understand what he was scribbling, writing until he collapsed, determined to expel it all. The fact that he understood nothing was beyond unimportant. The message was not meant for him.

He then transitioned to the dreamstates, albeit briefly. Which allowed him to describe Three's arrival, and the subsequent out-of-body experience, Darren observing as Three gave approval both to Darren's delivery and the work the trio were accomplishing.

When he finished, the woman sat there, her silent mask in place. Waiting. So he turned from the physics to the personal.

Darren didn't try to fit things into any semblance of order. He did as he had with Neil and the others. Giving tongue to the mental flow of images. When he reached the moments before Two's demise, he paused.

She remained intent upon the distant point where sea and sky merged. 'What is it?'

'I just remembered something. A flash of images. That's never happened before, this far after a transit. But it's so real now . . .'

'Skip the windup.' Spoken at just above a whisper, not so much gentle as intently probing. 'Tell me.'

'It started the instant Two, the feminine element, realized their enemy was on the hunt. She started her ascent, drawing them away.' He paused. 'I call her feminine because of the emotional qualities—'

'Doesn't matter. Not now. Two is the unit's feminine element as we describe in this day and age and culture. Got it.'

'She didn't drag me along. All three were with her in one sense, a lingering bond she tried to break but couldn't, not completely. So as she rose toward the city and her own death, she literally shoved these messages or images at me. Now when I think about that instant, I feel like she was trying to brand me.'

'Call them imprints.'

He nodded. Liking how they remained in sync. Even as he spoke about the impossible. 'Her unit, these four, are remnants of a vanished tribe. Or culture, or sub-race. All these words feel like they fit. When the ecological crisis struck, their tribe were blamed for the worst damage. Whether or not it's true no longer matters. It's become part of the modern legacy, a stain that defines those who are left.'

Darren watched a trio of gulls drift past, sailing with impossible grace in the blue-blue sky. Then abruptly the birds were gone, replaced by absent Two and her sacrifice to grant the others a few final few days on the forbidden planet.

'Only six of the floating cities still hold any of their tribe. They're kept around basically because it gives the leaders a safety valve. Every time the population rises to the point where a cull becomes necessary, they take aim at what's left of the tribe.

'My unit fled to this particular valley in the forbidden zone because it once marked the heart of their culture. Everything here held a special significance. Every rock, the cave where they live, the three waterfalls they're hiding behind, the light from dual suns, all of it. A lot of what they believed, or thought, whatever, it's all been lost. Nothing from that time has survived . . .'

He was abruptly gripped by a realization so intense his actual vision became vague and insignificant. He relived the instant of joining with the four aliens. This was no simple memory. It happened again, so intense he existed there. On the alien planet. In that incredible moment when they joined, these four, and invited him in. Then the alien he named Two was gone. The joining was fractured. The void she left was an acute vacuum that redefined all three of their remaining lives . . .

And suddenly Darren was weeping. Three chattering teenage girls were silenced and nearly frozen by the sight of Darren bending over his knees, convulsed by sobs. He cried so hard he could scarcely draw breath. The woman settled a hand on his back, patting softly. He cried harder still.

He fought against the choking torrent of sorrow. The futile wash of helpless defeat was so potent, it carried the risk of cutting off his breath. Darren gripped his knees so tightly his knuckles went pasty white. He wiped his face against one arm, then the other. Gasping for breath.

'Here.' She nudged his side. Harder. 'Take these.'

He forced himself back up, ignoring the looks passers-by shot him. They were the ones bothered by his emotions. Not him. Darren accepted the packet of tissues, cleared his face, blew his nose. He waited until his breathing was back under control, then said, 'Those poor kids.'

She glanced over, studying him intently now that he was back under control. 'Can I ask one more question?'

He wiped his face again, drank more from the bottle. 'You can ask anything you like.'

'Tell me more about these dreamstates.'

'Neil discounts their importance.'

A shift in the shadows alerted her to the female security's approach. The woman tapped her watch. The lady seated next to Darren waved her away and continued, 'Neil remains focused on the prize. Have you ever heard of the nine phases of civilization?'

Darren liked her manner, the importance she gave to their

conversation, the single-minded intent. Even discussing his dreams. 'Sorry, no.'

'The Kardashev scale predicts nine stages of planetary development. Most physicists, Neil included, think we're about three-quarters of the way to completing stage one. Full arrival would mean harnessing all energies of the home planet. Control of earthquakes, volcanoes, tornadoes. In the past, stage two has always been defined as harnessing the total energy of a star. Neil now believes that dark energy may provide us with an alternative source. Allow us to take a giant step toward higher ground.' She waved a hand over the beach, gesturing toward the future Neil envisioned. 'These new initial calculations redefine stage two. Neil is certain of this.'

Darren watched the female security speak with the driver, then start toward them. He briefly described how he had become increasingly certain the remaining three were all now connecting with him. He finished with, 'Anchali and Leila are having dream-states of their own. Anchali says she's received an invitation to transit. She thinks it means joining with my three.'

The woman followed Darren's gaze, nodded to her silent security, said, 'Does Neil know?'

'Leila says she's mentioned it. The idea makes sense. They know I'm not a physicist. It's possible they've accessed awareness of the others.' Darren hesitated, then added, 'My gut tells me there's a risk we don't see. Maybe it's because of Two's demise.'

'You're going to go back again. Transiting.' It was not a question.

'Definitely. The question is should we risk the others?'

'For the sake of humankind's advancement? My mind says absolutely.' She waited as he rose in stages, then offered her hand. 'But I've always had a healthy respect for gut checks.' She started toward where the security held open the SUV's rear door, then turned back and added, 'Contact me day or night.'

The female agent closed the woman's door, stepped forward, and told Darren, 'Go have yourself some lunch. The fish tacos are first rate. About an hour from now, look for a white Toyota Celica. That's your Uber.'

Darren remained where he was as the vehicle drove

away. Now that the conversation had ended, he felt immensely uncomfortable over how he'd broken down in public. He had only cried once during his late wife's long decline. It was not his nature to be defeated by remorse. He was a numbers guy. Expressing emotions, especially in public – and to a stranger – were just not his thing. He stood there long after the car had vanished, reknitting his world, trying to put the episode down to some very hard days.

TWENTY

Darren arrived back at the farm just after three. He spent the rest of the afternoon in segments. He worked a little, took two small walks, and after dinner did his best to stretch beyond his severely limited comfort zone. He held off the meds until the aches thundered. The unsettled feeling he had carried from his final moments on the boardwalk stayed with him.

Neil, Leila and Anchali gathered on the front porch just beyond his open window. Darren knew they expected him to join them, but he remained captured by the day and his time with the unnamed woman. He settled into his trundle bed in a room holding dusty fragrances of a bygone era. The drapes were closed, but he left the window open. He liked listening to the three of them talk softly, liked feeling part of work that defied the boundaries of humankind.

The only time they went silent was when heavy footsteps trod on the graveled path. Abbott. The colonel bade them a soft goodnight and kept walking. Only when his footsteps faded into the night did the three of them resume their soft murmurs.

Darren found it an excellent time to ponder the mysteries of this new phase. As in, how a man who only wept once at his beloved wife's departure could break down so completely and publicly in the company of a woman he did not know and might never see again. Over four aliens so far removed from his life the distance could not even be measured.

What was more, that same wrenching sorrow was still with him. Not as overwhelming as it had been on the boardwalk; the pain was a mere shadow now, compared to what he had experienced while talking with the mystery woman. Even so, it lingered, potent and dark as the open grave.

This was more than simply the agony over losing contact with an alien who had sought to help them. Who deserved better.

Darren felt bonded at some visceral level to the bitter fate that awaited all four of them . . .

Darren drifted into sleep. And almost instantly he was catapulted into a new dreamstate.

The brutish lead alien, their chief scientist, studied Darren intently. Four was immensely confused by Darren's ability to empathize. To actually feel sorrow over the loss of a nameless alien. The scientist seemed to be taken off guard by this realization. As if Four could not fathom how a thinking individual, someone whose professional world was built upon numbers, could also feel. It defied his concepts of life, of existence.

The alien scientist then delivered a message. There was no need for words. The sheer pressure of Four's urgency pressed at Darren with such force, he was hammered out of the dreamstate.

Darren rose to discover it was well past dawn. He forced himself to maintain his morning routine, washing and stretching and dressing. Only then did he carry the image out into their world. The alien scientist had pressed upon him a vivid image of the floating city, the place those four had once called home.

It hovered directly above their hidden valley. Hunting. Menacing. Their deadly foe.

The pressure to complete this joint mission was a terrible and growing force.

When he entered the kitchen, Fernanda turned from working the stove and saw something in his face that stifled her normal smile. They were all gathered around the table for once – Tanaka and Barry and the three scientists. And the colonel. The others, his lifelong friends, were effectively silenced by Abbott's presence. They ate with eyes fastened on their plates. They stared out the open rear door. They toyed with their mugs. Anything but look directly at the officer who had invaded their space.

Darren sipped from his steaming mug, feeling the internal burn rise to dominate his vision. The sensation was utterly new, and yet carried a very real sense of what he had just experienced in this latest dreamscape, and earlier, when he'd felt an entity return with him from the transit – so strong it threatened to suffocate . . . The chief scientist, Four, always carried an elephantine force. He dominated everything and everyone. The rage Darren felt building inside him was precisely how Four would have felt over having a barrier rise between him and his stated aim. Just like this man seated at their table. Abbott.

It felt better than good to take aim.

'What are you still doing here?'

The table did not freeze so much as simply shift directions. Multiple minds and gazes all had a direction. Abbott's gaze was the last to rise, as if the colonel sensed what was coming. And he resisted losing control. 'You're talking to me?'

'Of course I am. Don't pretend to be denser than you already appear.' Darren eased himself down into the lone empty chair. His battered state no longer mattered. He moved with the sinewy grace of a snake. Coiling. Taking aim. Showing the first hint of fangs. 'I told you yesterday what you needed to do.'

Abbott's smile was nothing but a contraction of his lips. '*You* told *me*.'

'Oh, excuse me. Did I not make myself clear?' Darren matched the officer's meaningless smile. 'Let's try that again. You show us you're on our side. That's your command, soldier. Your reason for being here. Now take a look at what happens when you *don't do your job*.'

Abbott's gaze frosted over. 'So now you think you're in command.'

'Pay attention to what's important. Look at the others. *Look*. Your job is to protect them, and facilitate our work. Protect. Facilitate. Do they look like they're working to you? No? Why? Because you're not doing your job!'

Neil muttered, '*Darren* . . .' But whatever he intended was stifled by Leila settling a hand on his arm. And squeezing. Hard enough to whiten her knuckles. Darren studied her. There was a new spark to Leila's gaze, a burning force she somehow managed to pass across the table.

'They don't trust you,' Darren said. 'Why should they? What have you done that shows them you're not linked to the group that nearly killed our friend?'

Abbott said, 'Obviously you're confused about the chain of command. I—'

'You're nothing,' Darren hissed. His words tasted like venom in his mouth. 'You *earn* your right to be here. Otherwise you're *gone*. Out of here. Now. Today.'

Abbott laughed out loud. 'Who let this guy out of his cage.'

'Let me clarify matters in words even you can understand.' Darren rose back to his feet. The viper coiling tighter and tighter. Fangs fully revealed. 'You bring verifiable evidence of who attacked us. Or. You. Leave. Now.'

Abbott's mouth opened. But something he saw in Darren's face silenced the officer. Perhaps also cut off his air. Darren didn't know and didn't care. The man was his now. And the table knew it.

'One more second of your putrid presence at this table, in this house, on our property, and I go public. I shout to the world what we're working on. Everything we've discovered, I present to the Chinese and the Russians on a silver platter. And I inform the Pentagon that it's all because of this *parasite,* this *enemy,* they've inserted into our ranks.'

When Abbott didn't move, Darren tossed his half-full mug in the officer's face. The nearly scalding liquid punched him from his chair. Abbott screamed an oath. He balled his fists and crouched. Mangling his curses, he was so enraged.

Then he spotted Leila. She held a cleaver and almost danced around the others who remained frozen in place.

Leila was then joined by Fernanda. The silent, ever-smiling chef had a butcher's blade in one hand, a slender filleting knife in the other. She had somehow managed to slip around the kitchen's periphery, almost within striking range.

Tanaka rose catlike, lifting his right leg high over the chair's back. His dark gaze held an identical killing glint to the women. He reached out to Fernanda, who handed him the filleting knife. The move was so smooth they might as well have been practicing it for days. Both gazes stayed locked on the officer. Their prey.

Abbott was utterly defeated by the sight. His battle-lust left in one shaky breath. He stood there, uncertain now. Confused. The only sound was that of coffee dripping on to the kitchen floor.

Leila hissed, 'Did you not hear the man, cabrón? You are not welcome here. You never were.'

Tanaka took another step, inserting himself between Fernanda and their prey. Arms raised, weapon ready.

Abbott shuffled past Darren on his way to the rear door. He opened the screen, then turned back.

Leila punched the air with her weapon.

Abbott fled.

A car started. The motor roared. Tires spun. Gravel flew.

Inside the kitchen, no one moved.

The car flew into the distance. Only when the morning sounds resumed, birdsong and breeze, did the kitchen come slowly back to life. Tanaka gathered their weapons and deposited them in the sink. Leila resumed her seat, then Tanaka. Fernanda walked over, took Darren's empty mug, and spoke calmly.

Leila said, 'She asks if you'd like breakfast.'

'Maybe later.' Darren remained standing as their placid chef recharged his mug. 'Right now, we need to get started.'

The others avoided his gaze as together they headed for the lab. He wanted to tell them the confrontation had been necessary to move things forward. They could not accelerate so long as Abbott was in the picture. But he remained silent as they entered the lab, completely astonished at his own outburst. The rage was so unlike anything he had ever experienced he could not even name it as emotion. This was something far more visceral. Darren took up an isolated position by the rear glass wall, well removed from Barry and Tanaka. They were all clearly uncertain how to respond to this new side of his persona. And there was nothing he could do about it.

Then Anchali called, 'Neil, my readings are all over the map.'

Leila said, 'We have to recalibrate.'

Neil and Barry and Anchali all glanced at him, as if worried Darren might use that as another reason to shout. When Darren remained silent, Tanaka asked, 'How long will that take?'

'Fifteen minutes,' Leila replied. 'Less.'

Darren decided if he was going to be isolated, he might as well go have breakfast. He re-entered the kitchen and accepted a warm napkin folded around a breakfast burrito scented with chorizo and fresh coriander. He recharged his mug and carried both on to the rear porch. He seated himself in a hard-back rocker that was shaded from the rising sun. He had never been any good at losing his temper. Rage had never been an emotion he'd been comfortable with. Darren watched insects flitter about, their wings turned to spinning prisms by the light. Normally losing his temper meant hours of remorse. Shame. Regret. This time, however, he felt . . .

Nothing.

The morning was windless, the heat and humidity a growing weight. Days like this, early summer when the coastal world held its breath, were a sign. Locals who watched the Florida seasons could read it as clear as a neon billboard. The beaches would soon fill, and the lifeguards would be hanging up the red triangular flags for dangerous rip currents. Tourists would ignore the warnings, drawn to the beautiful ocean by the heat and the joyous day spent doing exactly what they wanted.

But the locals knew. Oh my, yes.

Darren had spent countless days standing with his three mates and other surfers, watching the silent waters. Waiting. The stillness was a myth. The currents said it all. Out there in the distance, where the Atlantic dropped to depths beyond man's ability to explore, the world was undergoing a deadly change. A hurricane was building. Very soon the eye would form, and the raging tempest would take aim. It was only a matter of time.

His anger had not departed with the colonel. It lingered behind his eyes, coiled snakelike at the base of his spine.

Breakfast finished, Darren rose from the chair, returned inside and solemnly thanked Fernanda. He gestured at the position she had taken, in that molten instant when Abbott was shoved away. She accepted his gratitude with solemn silence, a shared moment. When she turned away, Darren returned to the front parlor and eased himself down on to the threadbare Persian carpet. He began another vague semblance of his morning routine. Giving his body something to do, while his mind revisited the confrontation with Abbott.

Reliving the moment his rage had uncoiled and consumed him. Searching for understanding. Such unbridled fury was simply not how he saw himself. His grim satisfaction when three friends confronted Abbott with knives, driving him from the room . . . Darren relived the moment and waited for some sense of repulsion, remorse.

What he felt most clearly was a lingering tenuous bond with

Four's dominant force. The alien chief scientist's power was so intense that this mere shadow, drawn from Darren's recent dreamstate, was sufficient to command Darren's own actions.

A phone rang, different from his own device – a quick, singular chime, pause, chime, pause. Darren rose to his feet, tracking the sound. Then he remembered the mystery woman and the bulky satphone she had handed him on the boardwalk. He walked to the parlor's corner table. The phone's console shone with a brief light that pulsed in time to the chime, a green square, no number, no ID. He touched the screen, said, 'Hello?'

'If your aim was to stir the hornet's nest, you've succeeded.'

Darren had a dozen responses. But he did not speak. His internal awareness was still active. He could actually feel the rage uncoil.

'Despite what you might think, the colonel's presence was necessary. He served a role. As long as he was present, your opponents inside the Pentagon and elsewhere remained content to sit back and observe. You and the team were safe—'

Darren's entire body arched, ankles to forehead, drawn into a near-rictus curve by the rise of fury that was not his own. Nor did it matter. Darren simply acknowledged the source. The power was totally consuming, racing up his spine, filling his brain, *demanding* to be released.

He did not speak.

He roared.

'How dare you sit in your office and lecture me about safety!'

Silence.

'Here's an idea. If there's a real threat, climb off your safe little perch and deal with it!'

He threw the phone across the room, barely missing the side window. Stood there as his muscles gradually unlocked, and this alien fury slithered down and recoiled at the base of his spine. Resting with a viper's calm. Waiting.

Darren returned to the kitchen, where Barry and Leila stood by the rear screen door. His friend asked, 'Who was that?'

He spotted an orphan burrito in the warming oven and headed over. He poured half a mug of fresh coffee, adding milk, wrapped a napkin around his second breakfast, and stepped outside. He waited for the pair to join him, then quietly replied, 'The contact

Mariana trusted with full reports. We met yesterday on the boardwalk. She didn't give me her name.'

Leila seemed amused. Barry looked concerned. 'You just shouted at Mariana's only high-level contact, our only trustworthy ally?'

'Yes.' He lifted the still-warm burrito. Took a bite. Delicious. 'Then I hung up on her.'

Barry asked, 'Was that wise?'

Darren leaned against the porch railing and met his friend's worried gaze. 'It was necessary.'

'You're sure about that.'

'Absolutely.'

'Can you tell us why?'

Another bite. 'No.'

Leila's reaction surprised him. She was utterly calm. For once her gaze seemed clear of all barriers. Her dark gaze rested calmly on him as she said, 'I came over to tell you the realignment is almost complete.'

Barry's concern deepened. 'Didn't Anchali tell me something about an irregular heartbeat?' When neither of them responded or even looked his way, he rapped knuckles on the porch railing. 'Hello, this is your landlord speaking.'

Leila went on, 'Anchali wants to do this. Transit. Try and connect with your unit. I feel drawn as well. But I'm still not sure.'

Darren finished his burrito before replying. There was a growing sense of two mental processes at work. The alien's rage was balanced against the individual Darren had spent years becoming. 'You and Anchali both need to answer one question before taking that step. What if the hunters find them? And either you or Anchali is connected when that happens?'

Leila paled.

Barry closed the distance. 'What about you? You're taking the same risk!'

'That's right, I am. And I've made that choice. The greater good is more important than the risk. Helping humanity achieve the next level. Ensuring our continued existence. Absolutely worth it.'

Leila demanded, 'You're saying that should be true for me as well?'

Darren searched her face, trying to find some hint of the former rage. And failed. 'You need to decide that for yourself. I can't tell you what to do.'

Barry remained where he was, blocking Darren from the stairs. 'Do you even hear yourself? You're risking your life for scribbles on a whiteboard! This is nuts!'

Darren felt the rage uncoiling from its position at the base of his spine. But this time he managed to suppress it. The awareness was incredible, even stronger than the rage itself. The newfound ability to balance and control the rage, borne from his lifelong affection for this good man.

On the one hand, he now possessed a force that rested and watched and waited. Everywhere his external eyes scanned, the alien force was there with him. Seeking the next reason to explode out. Strike. Destroy whatever stood between him and the objective.

On the other, he was still Darren Costa. The man who never lost his temper. It was like seeing the world through two different lenses. Darren wasn't certain how he felt about the dreamscape's aftereffects now being part of his waking state. All that had to wait. Because one issue was clear above all else. An element so potent he spoke the words aloud. 'Time is running out.'

Barry squinted, his face tight with a raw mix of concern and anger of his own. 'You can't possibly know that for certain.'

It was Leila who gripped Barry's arm, drew him back. 'Yes, he can.'

'What, because of some millisecond blast that might be nothing more than an electronic version of a pipe dream?'

'Yes, Barry. Exactly that.'

The merry jester of Darren's earlier years slumped in defeat. 'You are both acting crazy.'

As they started across the rear lawn, Darren glanced back to find Barry standing on the rear porch, dejected and confused and worried. As if in response, the burning power at Darren's core became cautious. Confused by how someone beyond their immediate unit, this four consisting of Darren and the three scientists, could maintain such a hold on Darren. An outsider who was far more than that. Darren looked back a second time, his internal vision heightened by the midday light and heat.

Darren stopped.

Leila asked, 'Everything OK?'

'Yes. Give me a moment.' He walked back to where Barry stood by the porch railing, helpless and frustrated and so worried he looked ready to weep. Darren looked up to this man, and saw anew the positive elements of their friendship. Not just the good times, but how Barry and Neil and Tanaka had all helped shape him into the person he was now. A man capable of controlling even this amazing moment. He said, 'Barry, you are a very good friend.'

The transition from blistering heat to the super-cooled warehouse, from brilliant sunshine to shadow, had an odd effect. Darren did not entirely focus upon his surroundings as he and Leila moved forward, through the semicircles of equipment, past Neil on his ladder, making final adjustments to the amplifiers while Anchali guided him, and into the cage.

He saw the floating city.

Neil looked down, said, 'We need a couple more minutes.'

'Good,' Darren told Leila. 'I need you to record this.'

She immediately moved to her station, touched keys, said, 'Rolling.'

'My last dreamscape was dominated by Four, The chief scientist.' He saw Barry enter the lab and walk slowly over to stand by the rear glass wall. He was tempted to stop and describe how the latest dreamscape's residue still lingered. But that particular revelation risked slowing their progress. And there simply wasn't time.

As if in confirmation, Neil lifted his hand and called, 'How is that?'

'Three degrees to your left.' Anchali waited while he whacked the amplifier with his rubber mallet. 'OK, that's good.'

'Test it at full power,' Neil said, and started climbing down. 'Go ahead, Darren.'

'What Two revealed has been built on by Four's new images. It's opened me to the true scope of danger facing them.' He could feel the static electricity building, the charge humming in harmony to the energy fueling his internal state. 'The act of their union resonated with everyone inside their city-state. They joined as four, but there is also a subtle secondary event, like a trace of this same unification that resonates through all the city-states forming their floating realm.'

He began pacing back and forth in the empty concrete expanse between the cage and the first line of equipment. 'This outlawed action is so incredible, it breaks so many iron codes, authorities inside the city-state were caught totally off guard. They discounted the first hints of this happening. No one believed it. And the same goes for their escaping and traveling to the planet's surface, the forbidden zone. They have remained safe this long simply because the acts are not just illegal, they're beyond comprehension.'

He stopped at the side wall, staring at the gray concrete, seeing the city-state hovering above their tribe's sacred valley. 'But the mask has been peeled away. That happened the instant they caught Two, and realized what was actually taking place. The city-state's entire power structure is united in a panic. If this was to get out, if the other city-states learned this has happened, they would be cast adrift. Everyone would pay the ultimate price. Condemned to the vacuum of deep space.'

He turned around, facing the frozen tableau. But what he really saw, the true focus of this intent, was his own internal vista.

The alien's rage and all it represented was in retreat.

Four's dominant force was gradually being erased. By the caring concern Darren felt toward these people, Neil and Barry and Leila and Anchali. And for an alien civilization. And for a fractured group who had invited him in. All of these part of his own life now. Bound to him through his ability to care deeply.

Leila called over, 'They don't know you've joined with them.'

'Your four have gone beyond the forbidden,' Leila said. 'Allowing you to become their friend.'

Darren allowed himself to be drawn back. There was one more crucial element he needed to share. Just in case he didn't make it back. 'Something else you need to know. The calculations that don't appear to be part of the usage of dark energy? They're not.'

The realization dawned in all three scientists almost simultaneously. Leila and Anchali rose and moved over, halting just outside the quantum cage. Staring wide-eyed as Darren continued, 'My chief scientist, Four, who's providing the data, was originally part of the team reaching out to the higher civilization. He was the scientist who had access to the city records and learned about the culling. He actually led a crucial part of their work, which he assumed had granted his unit the right to join, despite their heritage. Two, the earth mother who was caught and destroyed, she thought Four was wrong to try. But Four is the dominant force.'

For Darren, their rapt stillness held a power all its own. He had come to care for them in an entirely new way, these remarkably intelligent people and their quest to achieve the impossible. And there in the background stood Barry, his oldest friend, an anchor to all that had brought him here. He continued, 'But it was always just a matter of time before he and the others found themselves up for culling. Four now suspects the city-state's rulers were also hoping for a reason to exclude him from the scientific project. They loathed the idea of linking such a major discovery to this despised lesser tribe.'

Leila jerked back, as if avoiding a physical blow. It was Anchali who hissed, 'Those scum.'

They stood there, frozen in time and space, for far too long. Finally Darren said, 'We need to get started.'

Neil guided him into the cage, settled him on the plastic stool, and called, 'Are we counting?'

'Powering up,' Anchali said. 'Three minutes.'

As Neil lifted the cap with its crystal diodes, Darren asked, 'Is it absolutely, utterly necessary to have that thing dig needles into my scalp?'

Neil hesitated. 'Sort of, yeah. This is a fiber-optic hookup designed to monitor your brainwave and physical functions.'

Leila called over, 'Neil's toy gathers data for an article he'll never get around to writing.'

'That's totally not true!'

Anchali said, 'They'll never let you write this up. Or if you write it, you'll never see it published. Not in a million years.'

Darren heard the exchange, but mostly what he saw was three highly intelligent people who were prepping him for another trip. Concerned, aware, totally with him. He told Neil, 'It's OK.'

Neil remained standing there with the gizmo limp in his hands. 'There's no telling what this data might lead to, when we have time to really—'

'It's fine. Well, OK, not fine. Put it on anyway.'

The crystal-tipped diodes bit his scalp, as usual. Then, abruptly, it no longer mattered. Darren called through the cage's open door, 'Are you still recording?'

'Since the moment you walked in here,' Leila replied.

'I think the dreamstates have entered a new level,' Darren said, directing his words at Barry standing by the rear wall. 'This rage I've experienced, it's because of Four, the primary physicist and dominant energy of this group. He needs the other three to stabilize his existence. But now Two and all her caring, compassionate elements are gone. There is no barrier to Four releasing his full force. His domination of the group is now total. And this domination is impacting me on this plane.'

Leila said, 'You're still connected.'

Neil softly protested, 'That's impossible.'

Leila stood and yelled, 'Harmonic resonance! We've all suspected it holds a direct connection to second sound!'

'Theory,' Neil protested.

'Listen to what he's saying! Darren's just confirmed it! They're actually two faces of the same quantum coin.'

Anchali called, 'Ten seconds.'

Neil stepped from the quantum cage. 'Be safe.'

Anchali's calm voice sounded through his earpieces. 'Three, two, one . . .'

TWENTY-ONE

S*NAP.*

TWENTY-TWO

Once consciousness returned, Darren granted himself a few precious minutes on the gurney. Not long. Soon enough he was driven to his feet by what needed doing. Without delay.

He reached the whiteboard and began writing symbols and drawing graphic structures that held no meaning, at least for him. Nor did that matter. Darren remained somewhat disconnected from the frantic push to expel all he had brought back. He simply observed himself write with utter precision, forming line after line of a seemingly endless equation.

This time, Leila was ready when his hand cramped. She had prepared a mixing bowl filled with ice and water. While he soaked the aching digits, she massaged a spicy liniment into his arm from shoulder to wrist. Then she stripped off his shirt and did the same to his neck and spine. It was as close to an intimate moment as they had ever shared.

During that break Darren told them, 'This time it was totally Four, the chief scientist. I reached out to the other two, or tried, and Four gave me the equivalent of a slap on the wrist. Or a barked command. Something. Pay attention.'

When he was ready, Darren accepted a towel from Leila, dried off his hand and wiped down his arm and neck. He worked shirtless now, like some manic artist, filling three whiteboards. All the while, the trio stood by Darren's right shoulder, studying the inscription, silent.

Then it was over.

He stepped back and dropped his pen to the floor. Neil nodded, as if he'd been waiting for this moment to say, 'It's all beginning to make sense.'

Anchali glanced away from the whiteboard long enough to say, 'Explain that.'

'Nine stages of planetary development,' Neil said. 'Dark energy represents our first real chance to grow beyond stage one, if we can complete the formula to harness it.' He pointed to the whiteboards. 'This is all about the next stage – stage two. The aliens our contacts sought to learn from, they're already there.'

Leila said, 'Operating on a galactic scale.'

'That's what your chief scientist is offering us, isn't it?' Neil said. 'A clearly defined passage to our civilization entering even greater heights.'

Darren nodded. 'This is Four's revenge. Or vindication. Whatever. Giving away the biggest of their secrets. What leaders of his city-state spent generations trying to obtain. The same officials who reduced his tribe to secondary status. All of it handed to us as their farewell.'

Darren did not walk so much as drift through the super-heated afternoon, just another fleck of dust in the uncaring day. Leila remained so close he could feel her own heat, her strength. Every now and then a strong brown hand floated into his field of vision. As if she was aware of his need for a tether. Holding him to earth.

He wondered idly at the change in Leila. He didn't like to think that she saw his rage as all they shared. That his revealing a hidden fury was enough to remove her walls. Darren did not think so. Instead, he suspected it came down to his new bonds with their project. What was happening to him at a deep and mysterious level. Beyond logical explanation.

He had traveled numerous times to Mexico and Central America, first as a young surfer but also during his married life. He and his late wife had shared a fascination with the cultures and their roots in vanished civilizations. His wife had mastered both Spanish and several of the local dialects, a gift he did not share.

Occasionally between trips Darren had recalled something, a flash of memory so vivid it stopped him in his tracks. It pointed to a more profound level within these peoples, one he could neither identify nor put into words. But he often tried. His wife would hear him out, then always respond the same: There are aspects of life and human existence that defy our Western logic.

Just like now.

As he entered the parlor bathroom and emerged, Darren shared looks with the mercurial Leila. She stood in the doorway and watched him ease into the trundle bed. He hoped she felt this same deeper connection. But he was content with the thought that he might never know.

Darren's last view was of the woman's brilliant gaze.

Darren did not so much enter a dreamscape as become acutely aware that he slept. This sense of revised alertness granted him a clearer view of Four's latent power, a seed now planted deep inside his being.

The dreamscape's view shifted to observe first Leila, then Anchali. Darren watched, the outside observer, as Four studied the two with an intensity that bordered on fear. Four's power was on full display now, because its direction was not aimed at Darren. Instead, Darren watched as Four analyzed the pair, inspecting for something of vital importance. What this might be, Darren had no idea.

Then the chief scientist's attention shifted to Barry, then Neil. Gauging them, measuring their strength, their analytical ability . . .

Abruptly Darren was filled with a blinding flash of triumph. The incredible force was entirely Four. In that instant, Darren caught a very brief glimpse of an underlying motive. Not much, a mere fragment that suggested Four's desperate need, how he sought to determine what risk or threat the others represented. Something about this uncertainty had held Four back from . . .

Then Four became aware of Darren's own inspection. The dominant force took aim at him, a rage so potent it *shoved* Darren away.

Darren was catapulted into a fully awakened state.

The house was utterly quiet. Darren took his time rising from the trundle bed, used the bathroom, then went through a full set of stretches. His body seemed capable of resuming normal motions, not entirely, and not without serious aches, but he was definitely headed in the right direction. He dressed and entered the kitchen, where several pots simmered on the stove, filling the room with the perfumes of a fine meal. The coffee maker was also ready. Darren made himself a plate and ate and enjoyed the solitude. The food was delicious, a spicy blend of home cooking and distant lands.

He was midway through the meal when it hit him.

Four's latent power was gone.

His motions slowed, the final bites taken in careful stages. He looked around the kitchen, taking in the weather-beaten table and chairs, the scarred floorboards, the gentle wind blowing through the screen door. He felt as if he could breathe in time to the night. It was only now, when the dreamstate's aftereffects did not carry him forward, that he could see just how great an impact these alien visitations had foisted upon him. Because that was precisely the way to describe them. First the aliens had offered him a temporary pass, freeing him from burdens and emotions and the weight of dreadful memories. Then he had experienced Two's demise and witnessed firsthand the doom that awaited them all. Which had resulted in Four's power becoming fully unchecked. So great it shifted from dreamscape to Darren's earthbound reality.

The freedom resulting from Four's departure was exquisite.

Darren searched his internal space, the silence, the quiet mind. What he found was a renewed sense of self-identity. He had emerged from this encounter with Four possessing a new awareness of his own strength. For the first time since his wife's passing, Darren was able to look back, experience the full weight of loss, and not feel threatened by a renewed fracturing of his internal world.

The pain he still carried, the days and years he'd known with his late wife, the life they had built together, the professional existence he'd accepted because of her, all this shaped who he was *now*.

Darren sat at the kitchen table, looking at his empty plate, and missed his wife. His best friend and life partner. The hollow space she had once occupied was a void he would carry for the rest of his days.

And yet, this was a vital part of who he was. Did he truly want to give this up, leave behind the other side of that same coin, the love and affection and cherished memories of their years together?

He rose from the table, carried his plate and utensils to the sink, washed and dried them, then started out. The sunset was reduced to a pale wash over the western horizon. Darren crossed the rear yard, feeling ashamed at how far he had allowed himself to become involved in the dreamstate. And done so without questioning the cost.

He entered the lab, started across the concrete floor, then halted at the scene before him. Tanaka stripped plastic off a new whiteboard while Anchali stood by another, this one holding a few scribbled lines. Anchali held a felt-tip marker in one hand. But she wasn't writing. Her entire body trembled, as if she'd just run a terrible race, taking her to the edge of collapse. Even from his position by the glass wall Darren could see she was perspiring heavily.

He heard Neil say, 'It's OK.'

'It's not OK!' Anchali did not speak so much as wail. 'It's all right there! I can't . . .'

Neil showed her a parent's gentle and caring patience. 'You know how we always say – don't try and push out the images? Remember, Anchali?'

She looked at him, her face creased with confusion.

'You can't force this. Take a break.' He pointed to the gurney. 'You want to lie down again? You hardly rested at all.'

'No.'

'Fine. Let's just stand here a minute longer, see if it comes to you.'

'Why can't I make it work?' She held out the hand holding the pen, her fingers rigidly trapped in disjointed array. 'I need to *write*.'

'You will.' He moved in closer, settled his hand on her shoulder, spoke too softly for Darren to hear.

Darren did not realize Barry was standing a few feet away until he muttered, 'What a mess.'

Leila shifted from her position by the far corner, inserting herself between the two men. She told Darren, 'I should do this. Transit.'

Something about the scene, watching Neil gradually calm the scientist, filled Darren with an unease. He felt nervous worms crawl around his gut, but he had no idea why.

'I'm not helping,' Leila continued. 'Letting my fear dominate isn't getting us anywhere.'

Darren wanted to tell Leila not to take this step. Not to enter the cage again. That she was right to be afraid. But he could not shape the words.

Leila watched as Anchali lifted her arm while supporting that elbow with her free hand. She began writing, the symbols taking form with agonizing slowness. Leila said, 'I should go ahead and get the first one over with. Start doing some good around here.'

The calculations from his latest transit were there on the whiteboards to the left of where Anchali worked. Anchali's whiteboard held just six lines. Another to her right was totally blank. Waiting. He could almost hear the ticking clock. The hovering, hunting city state formed a shadow over his being. He remained silent.

Leila was the one who shivered now. 'All I can think of is my childhood, all the terrors creeping around me. It makes no sense, I know . . .'

When she went quiet, Barry asked, 'Where are you from?'

Leila jerked as if slapped. 'I don't know.' She glared at the man standing beside her, her rage back to the fore. 'I have no idea, OK? None.'

Barry held up his hands. 'Sorry. I didn't mean—'

She wheeled about, jammed her hands in her coat, headed for the door. 'I need a smoke.'

As she stormed away, Tanaka sidled up. 'What just happened?'

Barry stared at the slowly closing metal door. 'I asked her where she was from.'

Tanaka sighed. He started to follow her, then turned back and told Darren, 'Might be good if you could give me a hand.'

Darren followed him outside.

Night was settling on the world beyond the lab. Darren heard a new sound in the distance, the drum of yet more diesel motors. Leila leaned against the rear wall, drawing hard on a cigarette. The tip's glow illuminated the pinched and angry cast to her features.

Tanaka settled on the wall beside her. Darren stepped over to where the stubby concrete structure holding the lab's generators no longer blocked his view of the rear yard. Two full-size mobile homes stood by the distant fence, their illuminated windows casting an almost alien glow over the garden.

Tanaka said, 'I heard about you shouting at Evelyn on the phone.'

'Who?'

'Mariana's contact.' He pointed at the mobile homes. 'Six of her agents are now on around-the-clock rotation. Gary is our contact. We're supposed to ignore them.' He pointed toward the front yard. 'My team has pulled in closer. They've set up camp just beyond that first line of palms. Gary seemed to welcome their support, so they're here for the duration.'

'And Abbott?'

Leila snorted smoke and flicked her cigarette at the sand bucket serving duty as their ash tray. 'That clown is gone.'

'Permanently?'

Tanaka shrugged. 'Your guess is as good as mine.'

'We can hope.' Leila fished out another cigarette and flicked her lighter.

Tanaka asked her, 'You hungry?' When Leila did not respond, he went on, 'Fernanda has made us barbacoa de cabeza.'

When Leila remained silent, Darren offered, 'I have no idea what that name means, but it tasted fabulous.'

Tanaka asked her, 'When did you last eat?'

She pulled on her cigarette, shrugged.

'Why don't you go settle on the porch; I'll bring you a plate.'

In response, she took a final long drag, mashed her cigarette in the bucket, and headed across the rear yard.

Tanaka waited until she was inside the main house to say, 'Lady's got issues, sure enough.'

Darren could tell his friend what he'd been unable to say to Leila. 'There's something about connecting her and Anchali with my unit that's got my nerves on edge. The idea seems sound enough. And time isn't on our side . . .'

He stopped talking when the metal door creaked open and Neil followed Anchali out. The older woman did not even glance their way, just started across the yard, shoulders hunched, hands clenched by her side.

Neil called, 'You need my help?'

Anchali did not give any sign she had even heard.

Tanaka said, 'Darren's got the heebie-jeebies about the ladies making more transits.'

'Him and me both.' Neil settled on the wall beside his friend. 'Maybe I should have said something, tried to stop her. Oh, wait. I did. And look how much that accomplished.'

Tanaka's teeth shone briefly. 'You're not interested in following the lady's lead?'

'I haven't entered any dreamstate. I haven't felt any draw. I sort of wish I had.' He watched Anchali struggle her way up the rear steps and enter the kitchen. 'Almost as much as I'm glad it hasn't happened.'

Barry pushed through the door, checked to ensure Leila wasn't around, then asked, 'Should I apologize?'

'No need,' Tanaka replied. 'Let's go see if Fernanda's latest creation is as good as Darren claims.'

But when they entered the kitchen, Leila was seated at the head of the table. Her eyes were fastened on her plate as the fork rose and fell in slow, steady rhythm. Leila refused to meet anyone's eye, nor did she answer when Tanaka asked how the food was.

Neil asked, 'Where is Anchali?'

Leila used her fork to point at the front porch, then resumed eating.

All of them silently filled plates and left. Except Darren. He stood by the fridge, and waited.

When it was just the two of them, Leila lifted her gaze to his face. 'I need to do this. I have to.'

'I understand,' Darren said. And he did. The desperate appeal in her dark gaze silenced his worries. If he had something concrete to use as an objection, fine. But the woman was asking for his help, and he was going to give it.

She said, 'Time is not our friend.'

'No.'

'Or theirs.'

He nodded.

'Help me with Neil.'

'All right.'

She rose to her feet and stood there, watching him. Anger pinched her face into lines that were both alien and deeply imbedded. Finally she said, 'I knew I could count on you.'

The night was as close to idyllic as Florida came during hurricane season. The wind blew strong from the northwest, dry and strangely constant. A steady rush that whispered in the porch screen and flung the palms in a constant rattling chorus. Barry and Tanaka were seated on the front porch to either side of Neil. Anchali was there as well, tucked into the far corner, half-hidden by shadows. She did not rock so much as shift back and forward in tight little motions.

Neil was talking to Barry and Tanaka. 'There's a lot we don't know yet. But from what Darren has uncovered, their civilization treat second sound as a well-established and recognized portal. These new equations suggest that perhaps, just perhaps—'

'Here's a suggestion. Why don't you stop your unnecessary hesitations.' Leila's voice was not so much calm as featureless. Even so, it pierced the porch's calm. 'Go ahead and declare what we all know is happening.'

Neil's only response was to rock gently, back and forth, the chair's creaks an evening melody shared with the others.

Leila said it for him. 'We're working with three different sets of equations. Each represents a dimensional shift in human existence. The first is the incomplete one for dark energy. The second appears to be a form of anchoring this second-sound communication structure. Right now, we are hampered by our need to have a recognizable link on the receiving end.' She pointed to the sky. 'Either we build a receiver and send it into space, or we link with a planet where second sound is part of their own scientific development.'

When she went quiet, Tanaka asked, 'These new calculations erase those barriers?'

'Perhaps,' Neil said quietly. 'Perhaps.'

Leila looked at him, her gaze unblinking and copper-dark. 'We are viewing these new calculations from the perspective that other planetary civilizations are perpetually linked.'

Neil continued to rock and study the night.

Tanaka asked gently, 'And the third set of calculations?'

Anchali leaned forward, emerging partially from the shadows. She spoke with apparent difficulty, as if each word needed to be shaped individually. 'It's about lifting civilization to an entirely new level.'

Barry asked, 'Which civilization are we talking about here?'

Anchali's only response was to lean toward Leila and say, 'We need your help. This has to happen, and you know it.'

Leila shuddered. Shut her eyes. Shuddered again.

The porch was silent for a time, long enough for the moon to become a gentle spotlight rising above the nervous palms. The sky was so clear Darren could see the stars through the shivering screen. Finally Tanaka asked, 'Anchali, how are you?'

'Fine.' She had settled back into the shadows. Her voice was distant. Removed. 'Recovering.'

'She experienced arrhythmia, coming back,' Neil said.

'For ten seconds,' Anchali said. 'Less. Since then my heart has remained stable.'

'How could you possibly know the length of time it took for your heart to stabilize?'

Anchali held to that slightly fractured mode of speech. 'I know what I know.'

'Leave her alone,' Leila snapped.

Darren felt as if there were two different scenes vying for space on the porch. Maybe more. Leila trapped in a cage of her own making, wrestling with terrors and her past. Anchali refusing to acknowledge what toll the transit had taken. Darren and Tanaka and Neil, all of them serving as little more than an audience for the two women and their struggles.

Darren watched Neil shift his gaze toward Leila. The lovely young woman tensed, her entire body clenched in anticipation of a coming storm. He knew their coming argument was a total waste of a beautiful night. He said the first thing that came to mind, which was, 'Maybe I should transit. Now. Tonight.'

'Excellent idea,' Anchali said.

That shocked Neil from pressing Leila not to go. He swung back around. 'You were the one who said Darren needed to wait until tomorrow. That his heart—'

'Now, later, it is less important than the immense pressure we face.' Anchali rose in stages. 'The factor of passing time dominates everything. We must return to the lab and prepare for Darren's transit.'

Neil rarely lost his temper. On the few occasions when it happened, he did as he was doing now. Settling inside himself, voice dropping a full octave, the words falling like stones. 'Darren's next transit waits until tomorrow.'

Anchali replied, 'And I say—'

'Tomorrow. The matter is closed.'

Anchali held his gaze for a long moment, then silently left the porch.

Darren looked from one face to the other. He feared the team was coming apart, shredded by conflicting needs. The risk that their source would vanish was a reality. The threat they would never receive the required equations grew with each passing minute. The rockers' soft creaks might as well have been a multitude of ticking clocks, counting out their final chance. He knew Neil was right, wanting to protect him. But life was full of risks. He knew that better than anyone. He also knew death in and of itself was not the worst that could happen. He leaned back and stared at the moonlit vista beyond the porch, and remembered what it was like to stare into his wife's eyes as the light faded and she departed. Part of him had died with her. It was that simple. So what if he risked having his heart stop, taking another transit this soon after the last? Balanced against the chance to propel humanity into a new chapter . . .

Leila broke into his thoughts. 'I want to do this.'

Neil was still smoldering from his exchange with Anchali. His voice sounded like it emerged from a smoke-filled cave. 'Leila, tomorrow we're going to work with Darren, see what comes—'

'I want you to listen very carefully.' She rose to her feet. 'I am going *now*. Sit there and play boss long as you want. Anchali will handle it alone. Which only adds to the risk that has you frozen in place.'

She started from the porch, then looked down at Darren and said, 'It might help if you'd come with me.'

He hated being required to choose between his old friend and Leila. Just hated it.

Darren accompanied Leila around the house and across the rear yard. The satellite dishes rose like alien flowers, shadowy beasts opened to the stars. She slowed, then slowed further, until each step seemed to be taken against some great tempest only Leila could feel. Darren thought it was the perfect chance to express his concerns. But what were they, really? She knew as well as he did the risks imbedded in every transit. His own footsteps became mired in treacly doubts. But the words simply would not come.

He heard footsteps come up behind them. They were moving so slowly, he and Leila, the others were on them in no time. Neil and Tanaka and Barry, his three oldest friends, moving together down the path turned silver-white in the moonlight. Tanaka shifted his gaze to Darren, nodded once, then headed for the lab with Neil and Barry. Leaving the two of them to the wind and the night.

Leila was held by some force that twisted her features. Every step required an uncommon effort. She jerked in tight little fractional movements, staring blindly down the road gleaming pale in the moonlight, lined by shadow palms undulating in the wind.

She started weeping.

Darren asked, 'Leila, friend, what's wrong?'

Leila whispered, 'I'm terrified of dying.'

He responded from his own fears. 'Forget the transit, do what you do best. I'll go in the morning. Take what I bring back and make it live.'

She gave no sign she even heard him. Darren thought she stood like an injured puppet dangling from invisible strings. Her gaze never left the moonlit vista. She murmured, 'It's not a road. What I see in my dream.'

'You mean, in your dreamstate?'

She did not shake her head so much as shudder. 'What happened in the transit and the dreamstate only made it live for me all over again.'

She took a step away from the lab. Another. Darren followed and heard her say, 'In the dream I'm too little to know names. I feel hands holding me. Strong hands. I know these hands. And the voice. A man speaks. His words are the song I hear before falling asleep. Only I'm not sleeping now, and it's not a dream.'

She continued walking forward, as if drawn by the moon, pulled down the empty road toward a night populated by memories. 'I love the sound of his voice, so much I don't cry when he carries me into the silver water. It's cold, and I squirm, but he holds me, and everyone is quiet. Then there's a sound. Like thunder. A big hard bang. It is so sharp this sound, it strikes my ears. Crack, crack, crack. The hands let me go. I fall into the water. I can't breathe. It's dark and I'm moving and I can't find the hands.'

She stopped and turned and looked at him. She made no move to wipe her face as she said, 'If I'm lucky, this is when I wake up.'

Darren had no idea what to say except to repeat, 'You don't have to make the transit. I'll handle—'

'I've spent my entire life fighting those fears. Being strong because my papa's hands aren't there to be strong for me. It doesn't mean the fears are gone. They never leave. But I fight them just the same. Sometimes you have to fight even when you know the battle is lost. You have to be strong because that's all there is.' Her gaze searched his face, unshed tears reflecting the moon's silver glow. 'You understand, don't you?'

He wanted to deny. Deflect. But he couldn't lie. Not then. Not to her. 'Yes, Leila. I do.'

'Will you help me do this thing?'

'Of course I will.' He watched Leila take his hand, her fingers damp from wiping her face. 'I will talk with you and keep you company. I will remind you of my unit, and do my best to help you take proper aim.'

She squeezed his hand once. Good and hard. Then she released him and started back. 'Your hands never let go of your daughter, did they?'

'Leila . . .'

'Come on, Darren. Let's do this.'

They entered the lab to find Tanaka and Barry already standing by the rear wall. Anchali was writing another line of symbols on the same whiteboard as before, her features creased with intense concentration. Neil stood three steps back, one arm crossed over his chest, the other crooked so his chin could rest in the palm of his hand. The metal door clicked loudly as it shut. Anchali noticed Leila then. She capped the felt-tip pen and said simply, 'We should start.'

Obviously Neil had as many concerns and objections as Darren. Just the same, he walked to what was normally Leila's station and said simply, 'Powering up.'

'Alignment is one hundred percent,' Anchali said, so calm she sounded almost bored.

Darren followed Leila into the cage. He lifted the headgear off the floor and stood uncertainly until Leila reached over and set it in place. She positioned herself on the stool and watched him. Her dark gaze was so deep and somber it frightened him.

Through the open door he heard Neil say, 'Power stable at one hundred percent.' Then Anchali responded with, 'Ninety seconds.'

Leila said, 'Tell me where I'm going.'

Darren stifled all the myriad objections that fought to emerge. He swallowed hard and said, 'There's a home hidden behind three waterfalls. This isn't a cave. I thought it was at first. But their haven is surrounded by green, and it's more like an island hidden by the mist.'

'A hidden valley,' she said, intent now. Hearing him sparked something in her gaze. A fire, a determination, something. 'Got it. Next?'

'The three who are left, one is . . .'

'The professor. Right.'

Anchali said, 'Thirty seconds.'

'Three is a lab geek. Basically harmless, or so it feels.'

'And then there's Four,' she said.

He wanted to tell her to avoid Four at all cost. But Anchali started the ten-second countdown, and Neil called him to come out of the cage. So Darren stepped out and simply said, 'Come back to us.'

TWENTY-THREE

S*NAP.*

TWENTY-FOUR

Darren had never watched a transit before. Standing on the outside of the cage, witnessing Leila's body flash through the invisible lightning strike, was simply dreadful. The time involved was so tight it was unmeasurable. She left, she returned. Leila was already back.

Darren opened the cage's door as Leila spasmed. Her back arched so tight her face was almost pointed backward. Neil shoved him aside and rushed into the cage, there to catch Leila as she went limp.

Together the two of them got her on the gurney. Anchali drifted slowly over and started to apply the electrodes, but she wasn't fast enough for Neil. He shoved her aside and set the conductors in place, temples and forehead and neck and the skin over her heart. 'Strap her in. Keep it loose. It's just in case she spasms again.' He stepped to the readout machine, studied the thread of paper rustling out. 'Heart's strong. BP coming down. Her brain-waves are all over the map.' He glanced over, worried. 'Anchali, I can't remember, did she do this after her earlier transits?'

'Let me see.' For once the older woman was totally there. Intent. She studied the readout, decided, 'This looks good.'

Neil tried to read over her shoulder. 'Are you sure? Those pulses are wild.'

'I'm the expert here. And I'm saying she's good.'

As if in response, Leila's eyes opened. She struggled against the bands. Her expression reminded Darren of a fretful child. He stepped to the opposite side of the gurney from the two scientists and settled one hand on her arm. 'How are you?'

'I need to start.' She struggled to press against the belts. 'Get them off me.'

Darren thought her words now held the same disconnect as Anchali, like her tongue was too big for her mouth. Like she had to force her thoughts into vocal form. 'Maybe you should give it just a little time—'

Anchali snapped, 'Do as she says and release those straps.'

Darren did as she ordered, then helped Leila sit up. Anchali took her other arm, asked, 'Can you stand?'

'I need to, I want . . .'

'Good. Come with me.' She kept a firm grip on Leila's arm and led her to the next empty whiteboard. When Leila squinted in confusion at the blank space, Anchali lifted her right hand and gave her a felt-tip pen. 'Ready?'

'I . . . Yes.'

'Good.' Anchali stayed where she was as Leila began writing. Her movements were unsteady, the symbols so scrawled Darren wondered if anyone could actually read them. Just the same, Anchali seemed satisfied. She stepped to her own half-filled whiteboard, uncapped another pen, and resumed work.

Darren stepped over to where Tanaka and Barry remained by the rear wall. He stayed like that for over two hours. The two women kept silently working their whiteboards. Twice Leila's hand gave way, and the second time she scrawled a long black snake down to where the whiteboard's bottom shelf caught her. Neil started forward, but Anchali snapped at him, 'I have this.'

The older woman murmured softly as she held Leila's arms, positioning her before the whiteboard. Anchali asked softly, 'Do you need water, food, rest?'

In response, Leila gathered herself and resumed working.

Anchali wiped away Leila's initial snakelike scrawl, then glared at Neil before resuming her own work.

Neil stood behind the two women, confused and worried. Darren agreed with him. Anchali's reaction made no sense. She had gotten her way, Leila had taken the step, the two of them were working in tandem. What made Neil the bad guy of this story?

Finally Darren's fatigue got the better of him. He forced his legs to carry him back across the yard. He climbed the porch stairs and crossed the kitchen and entered the parlor and dropped on the bed.

He lay for a time, recalling those final days in the hospital with his beloved. He'd grown accustomed to living under the weight of fatigue. In those hard days and nights, exhaustion and bodily stress had simply been another bitter component of admitting defeat. He'd given into the weariness when he felt sleep was possible, even when rest left him feeling guilty. Wishing he could instead remain at her bedside, day and night, seeing to her every need. Making sure she had everything possible to ease her passage through the dread hour. He couldn't save her life. So he would do what he could. Be there. For her. He had learned to sleep on floors, in chairs, even stretched over the hard benches lining hospital corridors.

He found a subtle comfort in how, for the first time ever, such a recollection did not pierce him with sorrow's blade. Instead, he fell asleep worrying if these recent transits to his own fractured unit might have wounded his two new friends.

Darren woke an endless time later to find someone had covered him with an Indian blanket. They had also opened a window, and a cooling dawn breeze drifted in from the northwest. It was the rarest of winds during the run-up to hurricane season, dry and fresh and filled with the incredible fragrance of orange blossoms. Darren drifted for a time, then fell back asleep.

When he woke up a second time, the sun was a strong presence, flashing against the gauze curtains and filling his room.

The dreamstate had not returned.

His body had stiffened during slumber. He had not taken any meds the previous night, and he felt it now. But as he walked in slow careful steps toward the bathroom, Darren had a distinct impression of steady recovery. He decided to put off the morning meds until he absolutely needed their comforting presence, and began his stretching routine. Pushing himself closer to his standard limits, even though the muscles and ligaments strained by the attack grew irritated and complained. But he had been through worse. He knew precisely what needed doing, the gradual movements, the slow increase of motion until he was into full stretches, breathing deeply, ready for the new day.

Or so he thought.

Darren showered and stretched a second time. There were some distinct aches that he suspected would need treatment before the day was over. But just then it felt beyond good, starting his day with a clear head.

He dressed and entered the kitchen. Fernanda greeted him with a charged mug and held up the skillet. He smiled, nodded, asked please in Spanish so awful she actually laughed.

The wall clock read a quarter to nine. The generators behind the lab hummed full bore. Darren assumed it meant one of the women had made another transit. He did not like the idea, but his frustration was more muted now. Both had gone, come back, done what appeared to be solid work on their respective whiteboards. At least Neil had found no reason to complain. Darren remained troubled, but he saw no reason to say anything more.

He was midway through a second portion of Fernanda's huevos rancheros and a third mug of her strong black coffee when the screen door opened and Neil stepped inside. He wore his somber expression, the one where the world seemed to drag everything downward – features, shoulders, gaze. He smiled at Fernanda's offer of coffee and spoke to her in Spanish, then asked Darren, 'How are you?'

'Better than good. Ready to go.'

In response, Neil retreated to the door, pushed it open, and waited for Darren to rise and thank Fernanda and carry his mug outside. As they crossed the rear yard, Neil said, 'Leila made another transit this morning.'

Beyond the satellite dishes, Darren spotted two of Evelyn's team standing by the door to the nearest mobile home. He raised his mug in greeting. 'And?'

'She knew I was against it. So she and Anchali did it on their own.' He flung his hand in the lab's general direction. 'She's still on the gurney. Anchali keeps saying she's fine.' He cast Darren a worried glance. 'I just don't know. Maybe we should wait.'

'We can't.'

'Darren, you haven't seen how she looks. She isn't moving.'

He stopped where the sunlight struck him full in the face. Darren liked the heat, the way it seeped through the aching muscles, all the way to his bones. He breathed around the conflicting thoughts, a jumble so tight with nerves it was hard to make sense.

Neil asked, 'Why are we stopping?'

Darren took a careful sip. 'You're one of my oldest friends, and I admire you more than I could possibly say. I know where you've come from, and I know what you've done with your life. So I'm giving it to you straight. I feel like there are these two different storms brewing inside my head.'

Neil's response surprised him. He stepped back, stared up at the sun, used the fingers of both hands to rub his wiry silver-black hair. And he laughed. Then, 'Man, you don't know, you can't imagine, how good it makes me feel to hear I'm not the only one.'

'One the one hand, we've got two ladies who haven't been totally OK since Anchali took her transit yesterday. And now Leila is on the gurney, and you're stressed because you came to get me so I can go in there and do the same thing.'

Neil was squinting. And grinning. And worried. All he said was, 'You're on a roll. Don't stop now.'

'On the other hand, we know full well our sources are about to be . . .'

'Expunged,' Neil offered.

'That works.'

'Which means we're under huge pressure to go full bore,' Neil said. 'Despite how the risks make me so tight I haven't kept a meal down for what feels like weeks.'

'How is the work Anchali and Leila brought back?'

'Just incredible. Game-changing material.' Neil kicked at a loose pebble. 'But slow. Together what they've managed to get down is maybe a fifth of what you brought back last time. Less.'

'So there's your answer.'

'You sure about that?'

'Yes, Neil. And at one level, so are you.' Darren started toward the lab. 'Let's get this over with. The absolute last thing I want to have happen is for the rest of my alien unit to be captured while I'm joined up.' Darren could tell Neil wanted to continue arguing, and knew it was utterly futile. So he changed the subject. 'The dreamstates have stopped.'

Neil slowed. 'Since when?'

'Basically since Anchali transited.' Darren grabbed Neil's arm and pulled him forward. 'I don't know what it means. But I think . . .'

'Tell me.'

'My unit has become totally focused on our gaining access to all three equations.' Darren reached for the door. 'Their situation is too time critical for sidebar elements like these dreamstate connections.'

Whatever Neil was about to say was halted as soon as they stepped into the lab's cool wash. It was just the four of them now – Barry and Tanaka were gone. The two women worked side by side, filling a pair of whiteboards. Neil brightened immensely and called over, 'Leila, how are you?'

'Leila is fine.' Anchali glanced over. 'Darren, are you going?'

Neil started toward Leila, clearly intending to check on her state. But he halted when Anchali aimed the hand holding the pen in his direction. Not so much angry as hostile. Her gaze was a blank wall. 'Allow Leila to focus on the work.'

Darren thought Leila looked beyond frail, a parchment copy of the normally vibrant scientist. But the previous day's scrawled writing was replaced by work so precise it could have been laid out by a machine.

Anchali said again, 'Leila is fine. Are you going?'

'Right now.'

'Right now is good. Excellent in fact.' She headed for her station. 'Everything is still set up from Leila's transit.'

Darren hesitated a long moment, then started toward the cage. The lab's fractured atmosphere troubled him greatly. The same concerns that had drawn him from sleep were here in this space. He settled on the stool, wishing he had taken his morning meds. Set the chemical blanket in place around his brain and body before they shot him off to never-never land. He sighed. Too late now.

Neil followed Darren into the cage. He must have seen something in Darren's expression for he said, 'Give me the word, we'll call this off.'

Darren glanced over to where Leila slowly formed another line of symbols. The woman had not looked once in his direction.

Darren was not so much determined as resigned. 'Let's do this.'

Anchali looked up, met Darren's gaze, nodded once. 'Thirty seconds.'

TWENTY-FIVE

S*NAP.*

TWENTY-SIX

Darren must have blanked out for quite a while, long enough for Neil to shift from deep concern to borderline frantic. He wasn't shouting, not really. 'Come on, Darren. Don't do this to me.' More like struggling to find enough air to speak at all. Then he noticed Darren's eyes were open. 'Hey, bud, there you are.' Neil sounded like he was ready to weep. 'You gave us quite a scare.'

'You are the only one frightened.' Anchali stood by the monitors, studying the readout. She sounded bored. 'I told you he is fine.'

Neil looked over, his face screwed up in confusion, as if not certain who spoke. Darren reached for Neil's arm, took hold and pulled himself upright. Instantly Neil turned back and used his other hand to support Darren. 'You sure you're ready?'

'I'm OK.' Strangely enough, he was. As his vision cleared, two immediate impressions struck him. The first was Leila remained as she had been before his transit. She worked the whiteboard, each symbol being laid out with careful precision.

The second was more personal. Four's dominant force had returned.

Only this was a different experience from before. The incredible sense of power was not content to rest dormant in his gut, waiting for a reason to strike. Four's energy was no longer latent. Instead, it held a fierce totality. So strong it began shouldering Darren aside. Taking full control of his consciousness.

Darren rose from the gurney and started toward the whiteboard. Anchali took hold of his left arm, knowing without asking that he needed her support. His legs, his body, were no longer under his control. And she knew it.

Neil said something, but there was neither room nor interest in anything the man said. He was no longer Darren's friend since childhood. Neil had abruptly become a stranger. Of no importance, save for how he would never serve as conduit for Two. The member of their unit who was no more.

Anchali spoke one word. 'Leila.'

Instantly she left her whiteboard and started over, her steps jerky, her motions highly uncoordinated. All this had a name now, a reason. Darren knew, and yet he was helpless to do more than observe. He did not struggle against the sensation of being shouldered aside. There was no longer even an ability to feel helpless. This was the new status.

Four was taking over.

The two women positioned him in front of the next empty whiteboard. Darren – or rather, what was left of him – watched as his right hand fumbled with the pen. The motions of his fingers were erratic. He was unable to move his two hands together, even find the coordination to uncap the pen. Anchali understood. She fit one of her hands around his, used the other to take off the cap, then positioned the hand by the whiteboard's left-hand corner. All the while, Leila gripped his left side, using all her strength to keep his body upright and steady.

He began to make slow, jerky notations. Darren realized now there was a second and far more important purpose to the act, a secret that lurked within the grim and determined attitude the three of them now shared. The act of inscribing calculations formed the conduit. All the while, beneath this cover, Four continued to shove him aside, striving for full control of his being.

The women remained tightly linked, Leila gripping his left arm, Anchali one hand at the base of his neck, the other holding his writing arm in position. Bonded to him and the moment of Four gaining full control. Darren felt both their breaths on his face. The heat formed another factor in this struggle of transition, one life ending while another became dominant. Three lives from another world. Here and in sync and alive.

Neil spoke again, but he was at some huge distance now, attached to an individual who was gradually fading to nothing.

Darren felt himself being compressed and squeezed until his body's actions, standing and writing and breathing and living, gradually drew further and further away, until he became as inconsequential as Neil.

He felt a miniature *snap*, a fragile repetition of the transits, and knew his life and time on earth was being severed.

Between one breath and the next, his heart stopped.

In that fractured instant, Darren found himself able to observe Four, this being who he now assumed was in total control.

Four had never experienced pain before.

Pain was an experience that did not exist on his home planet.

The utter alienness, the sheer overwhelming force of agony, expelled Four.

In that final instant of torment, Darren glimpsed the alien hovering there beside him, a faceless entity shaped vaguely like Darren's own physical form. Then the cloud began to splinter. Four might have shrieked at his demise. Or perhaps it was merely Darren's response as he resumed control of his body. Just in time to experience his coming death.

TWENTY-SEVEN

Darren woke up inside an ambulance.

Flashing lights reflected about the rear cabin where Darren was strapped to a gurney. The instant he opened his eyes, Darren felt a pressure ease off his chest. Blue-gloved hands lifted up, and a woman's face moved in close. She shouted through her mask, 'Sir, Darren, can you hear me?'

He nodded, or tried to. Un-gummed his lips. Tried to speak.

One hand settled on his bare shoulder. The woman turned toward the front compartment and shouted words he could not be bothered to understand.

A sense of life-or-death urgency filled him. Darren's brain refused to clear. He knew there was something he had to do, a vital need that simply could not wait. But he couldn't make his brain form a decent thought.

The woman attendant saw him shift about and gripped his shoulder more firmly. 'Take it easy! Sir, calm down!'

Darren's mind cleared a fraction further, enough for him to hear the driver shout, 'They ask if the patient is intubated!'

'No need. Turn off the siren.' In the ensuing quiet, Darren felt the needle inserted in his arm. The woman was calmer now. 'Patient is breathing normally. But he's clearly in distress. Tell them I'm adding five mil of morphine to his drip.'

Darren felt the icy liquid flow into his arm, almost familiar now. There was a very brief instant of clarity, long enough for him to lift his head and peer down the cabin's length. Then the blue-gloved hand settled on his forehead and pushed him back down.

One glance was enough.

Anchali and Leila rode in the back with him. They shared the narrow drop-down bench with a man Darren did not recognize. Darren stared at the ambulance's metal roof, the exterior lights flashing on-off, on-off. He decided the man had to be one of Evelyn's agents.

Soon as the attendant's hand released him, Darren lifted his head for another quick look. The man wore a holster on his belt. His gaze shifted from Darren to the driver to the road ahead, to the two women sharing his bench, and then back to Darren.

The two women only had eyes for him.

The attendant pressed his head back down.

Darren felt his blurred and pain-wracked state begin to fade. He was strapped to the gurney, held tight by a band across his chest and another holding his legs. Padded leather straps bound his wrists to the steel supports. He was utterly helpless.

As the morphine drew him away, Darren had time for one utter certainty. His two friends had been shoved aside. Just as Four had almost succeeded in doing with him.

Anchali and Leila were no more.

Their flat gazes said it all.

Soon as they realized Four was gone, they would eliminate him. It was their only chance to remain safe and undetected. Darren had to go.

TWENTY-EIGHT

Darren dreamed he was floating in a warm Caribbean sea. He was seated on his old board, his favorite from a different era. The familiar fragrances brought the moment into beautiful clarity, sea and board wax and sweet tropical breeze. He was unable to see much because he faced straight into the rising sun. He lifted his right arm to shield his eyes, and waited for an incoming wave.

He could see another couple of surfers over to his right. It felt so good to share this incredible moment with friends.

Then he felt a piercing worry. Where were Anchali and Leila? Darren dropped his arm, swung his board about, searched . . .

He woke up.

Full awareness brought with it the hospital room's astringent odor. It was a distinct flavor he recalled from his many earlier episodes. He took his time assessing his situation, keeping his eyes closed long after his thirst pushed at him to come fully awake. He felt the intravenous drip attached to his arm, the monitors fastened to his chest and temples. He had much to think about, but what held him tightly was bone-deep regret over how he should have seen this coming.

The sound of someone trying to be quiet, shuffling their feet, coughing softly. The unseen threat forced him to open his eyes.

Neil stood beside his bed, on the side opposite his various medical attachments. At a motion from Darren, his friend held the cup where Darren could fasten on the straw. The taste of ice-cold liquid was purely exquisite.

When he was done, he asked, 'Where are Leila and Anchali?'

'They're just outside.' He set the cup back on the side table. 'They wanted to be here, but I needed to have this time alone so I could apologize.'

'Neil—'

'Let me finish. Please.' A hard breath, then Neil launched in with, 'I alone am responsible. This was a serious lapse in my professional judgment.'

'Listen—'

'I almost got you killed. And for what?'

'For a lot. Neil, please, you really—'

Anger flashed on that normally placid face. 'Is it so hard to give me a second?'

'The woman who handles the agents. Evelyn. I need—'

'That's it?' Neil was so angry now he rammed back from the bed, struck the wall, ricocheted toward the exit. 'I've spent all night outside your room, hoping for one chance to say how utterly distraught I am, sorry beyond words for risking your life by getting you involved, and all you can say is to go find a stranger?'

'Wait, this is urgent—'

Neil did his best to fling the door open, but was defeated by the pneumatic hinges. 'Find her yourself!'

Darren spied the agent seated outside his door. He was fairly certain it was the man who had ridden in the ambulance, but couldn't be sure. The agent glanced in, curious but not alarmed. Darren lifted his arm, started to call in the agent . . .

Too late.

Leila and Anchali crowded in. Their arrival was a continual flow meshing with his friend's angry departure.

Darren's request died unspoken. His arm dropped back to the bed. Defeated.

Anchali pressed the door fully shut, then joined Leila at the foot of his bed.

Leila wasted no time. 'Our partner did not make it.'

'No,' Darren said. The desire to lie was futile. His fate sealed. 'Well, he did. But my heart attack shoved him out.'

Anchali glanced at the other woman and told her, 'Partner is a feeble word for the one we have lost.'

'Partner has multiple definitions.' Leila spoke to Anchali while holding Darren's gaze. Her eyes were flat, blank, emotionless. 'One meaning is a beloved unit not formally joined in legal marriage.'

They wore Leila's and Anchali's faces like wax masks. The eyes were what Darren found most frightening. They observed him with an indifference that spelled his doom.

Anchali conceded, 'I suppose the word partner suits. A bit.'

'The language is rudimentary, I agree,' Leila said. 'Spanish is little better. And Thai?'

'Older. Somewhat more nuanced. Not much.'

Darren asked, 'Who is carrying who?'

'Whom,' Anchali said. 'Your own language is precise on at least this point.'

'Which means you've got to be the professor. My first connection.' Darren looked at Leila. 'Which means you're carrying the science geek.'

'Carry is hardly the proper term,' Leila replied.

'It doesn't matter.' Anchali started around his bed.

Leila followed closely behind. 'Or rather, it will not matter much longer.'

The bathroom door opened and Evelyn leaped out. 'Step away from the patient. Gary!'

The outer door instantly opened. The agent stationed outside his door entered. The hand not opening the door swept around, holding a weapon Darren did not recognize.

Evelyn snapped at the pair, 'I gave you an order.'

'An order,' Anchali said. 'Interesting. And precisely why—'

Darren spotted Leila's hand emerging from the back of her blouse. He and the agent shouted together, 'Gun!'

Evelyn drew her own weapon with fluid swiftness as Gary fired at Leila. Evelyn shot Anchali. Neither weapon made any sound. Then Darren heard an electric *snap*.

Both women jerked in nearly identical spasms.

Evelyn shouted, 'Again!'

Their free hands drew two more stun-guns. Both fired simultaneously.

The women dropped.

Evelyn's first gun beeped a recharge. She leveled it and waited as Gary knelt and checked them both. He glanced back. 'They're gone.'

'That's not possible.'

'I'm telling you, they're both dead.' He checked his weapon. 'Set to stun. You?'

'Same.' She stepped closer. 'Try again for pulses.'

He did so. 'They're dead, boss.'

Darren sighed, sorrow and relief in equal measure. 'That matches with what happened to me.'

'Explain,' Evelyn snapped, still aiming at the women.

Darren described his return from the final transit, Four shoving him aside, then his heart attack and the alien both repulsed and expelled by its first experience of human pain.

'I guess that works.' Just the same, Evelyn kept her weapon raised as she said, 'They knew you weren't one of them.'

'I'm pretty sure they realized Four was gone while we were inside the ambulance.' He studied two prone bodies. 'I'm so sorry.'

'Don't be.' Evelyn finally holstered her guns. 'It saves us having to make a terrible choice.'

Gary pointed one of his weapons at Darren. 'Can we be certain about this guy?'

'They were about to kill him.'

'They said that?'

'No question.' Evelyn inspected Darren. 'Something else. The first thing he did upon awakening was to ask for me.'

Gary showed a genuine reluctance. 'I guess that works.'

'He's not one of them,' Evelyn insisted. 'Holster your weapon.'

An hour later, Darren watched Gary and another agent bundle the two women into yellow hazmat postmortem bags. Their actions were observed now by hospital security, an off-duty policewoman, and various hospital staff.

And Neil.

At Evelyn's direction, nurses and orderlies shifted Darren's bed into an adjoining room. He knew he should probably say something to Neil. But even as he passed his horrified, mortally stricken friend, Darren remained mute. His mind and body were too full of a toxic mix of regret, relief, remorse. So many mismanaged cues. So much he should have done better. All the events since returning to his homeland, working so hard to help his oldest friends, and he was rendered as empty and defeated as when he left Ohio.

Once they positioned him in the new chamber and refastened his monitors, Darren refused their offer of food, turned his face to the wall, and fled the only way left to him.

TWENTY-NINE

Six days later, they drove him from the hospital. Evelyn rode in the Tahoe's rear seat with Darren. Gary and another agent he did not recognize were up front.

Evelyn had stopped by his room three days earlier. But Darren was still processing, and they did not speak. She had seemed to accept without discussion that he needed more time. Once she departed, Darren had wondered how many other times the woman had observed people returning from clandestine missions that had gone horribly wrong.

The next day, they refused him permission to attend Leila and Anchali's funerals.

Tanaka stopped by on his way to the service, his visit monitored by Gary, the agent. Orna was ordered to remain in the corridor. One visitor, one time. Tanaka was dressed in a dark suit, his hands fumbling with the confusion that creased his features. He was clearly having difficulty understanding what had really happened. Darren refused to explain. He only spoke to ask how Neil was faring.

Not good was the answer.

They left the Melbourne hospital, crossed the Intracoastal Waterway, and headed south along A1A. Darren knew the lady was waiting for him to speak. And he had questions that definitely needed answers.

'How did you know?'

She turned in her seat, her entire body sweeping around. As if she had been waiting all this time for him to utter those precise words.

Darren went on, 'You were waiting in the hospital bathroom for a purpose. You already suspected. You needed to be sure.'

'I didn't know anything for certain,' Evelyn agreed.

'But how?'

'The man I met on the boardwalk, who broke down over the

fate of four individuals he would never meet,' Evelyn said. 'That was not the man I knew from your file.'

He repeated slowly, 'Not the man you *knew*.'

'That is a major portion of my remit. To know people and determine what about them is true. Your emotions that day were real enough. But they didn't mesh with someone who did not weep at his wife's funeral.'

He did though. Inside. 'That was in my file?'

'Of course not. But I was concerned. So after our meeting I went back and I asked.' She offered a very thin smile. 'You know what happened next.'

'I yelled at you on the phone.'

'You raged at me,' she corrected. 'Again, utterly without precedent. So I wondered. And sent Gary and his pals to monitor the situation. They set up cameras and listening devices throughout the property. Which were fried every time they amped the power up for another transit. I insisted they go back and replace the devices soon as you vacated the premises. We all saw how the ladies changed.'

He sorted through a variety of responses, most of which were laced with his guilt for getting such life-crucial elements so wrong. In the end, though, he settled on asking another question. 'Do you have any idea who was behind the attacks? I mean, when Leila was accosted outside the bar, then the car—'

'I know what you mean. And the answer is these weren't attacks. Not really. Call them what they were. Probes of your defenses.'

'I don't understand.'

'They were probes,' she repeated. 'Nothing more. Your opponents were checking for weaknesses.' She hesitated, her head bobbing in time to some internal debate. Finally, 'Perhaps it's time we discussed the underlying elements. Consider this, Darren. Colonel Mariana Alveraz, my friend, served as a crucial buffer. They needed to know if she was truly as she appeared. An observer put in place by Canaveral's military arm at DARPA's request. There to make sure the money was correctly spent and the scientists behaved. These probes were designed to reveal who else was involved.'

'The opposition made these probes because they were looking for you?'

'If I'm correct, yes. Your opponents were desperate to learn how high up the food chain you and this project are connected. Knowing this answers another even more vital question.' She waited.

This time the answer hovered in the heat beyond their windows. 'How worried they need to be.'

'How serious are the top decisions makers in Washington treating Neil's work,' she confirmed. 'Very few DARPA projects receive the sort of attention this one has. One in a hundred. Less. If they knew this connection existed between you and me, *then* the attacks would begin.'

'So who do you think were behind these probes?'

'There are multiple possible answers to that question. I have my suspicions. Tight fragments of evidence. Nothing conclusive. At this stage, the one thing I can definitely tell you is this: the further you and your team proceed down this path of discovery, the more corporations and nations will view you as a serious threat.'

'When you know who was behind the attack, will you tell me?'

'Once we have conclusively identified them, yes.' She paused, then added, 'But only if you are still involved.'

'You want me to take over Mariana's position. Be the go-between.'

'Will you?'

He took his time responding. Long enough to recall the initial dream that split his burdened former life from whatever came next. A breath, another, then, 'Yes.'

'You understand what I'm asking. The risks.'

'Not fully,' he replied. 'But enough.'

'In that case, I'd like to offer you an official position. Administrative director of DARPA's newest division. Excellent pay and benefits, all backdated to your start on this project. If the day ever comes when you're ready, we can happily reassign you to a number of other projects where your talents would be most welcome.'

* * *

They did not speak again until her driver parked by the Melbourne Beach boardwalk. Darren spied his friends gathered, perhaps at the same bench where they had met all those eons ago. Orna was with them now. And Mariana, staring out to sea from her wheelchair.

Darren asked, 'What do I do now?'

'That brings us to my purpose for being here. Neil needs your help. Desperately. Now more than ever.'

'I'm not a physicist.'

'We'll find him a suitable associate. Or two. What he needs is someone he fully trusts who can keep him anchored. Hold him to a definable course.' When Darren did not respond, she added, 'There's a great deal more work to be done here.'

Darren nodded. It made sense. 'You're keeping us at the farmhouse?'

'I like the sound of that word, Darren. Us. I like it very much. The answer is, you can go anywhere you like. But that location has a great deal to offer. Go talk it over with your friends. Take your time. Decide.' She smiled as she handed him another satphone. 'Please try and hold on to this one a little longer.'

They were all watching his approach, everyone save Neil. Mariana's head was bandaged and one leg was in a full cast. But her eyes were clear and she managed a smile.

Darren felt mildly numb, returning to the point where this remarkable journey had begun. Several of them, in fact. From the purple-painted youngster off to Ohio, then back and off again, this time to a distance that truly defined unmeasurable. Especially since they had no idea where he had actually gone.

Evelyn's Tahoe drove away, a silent beast from some alien world. But Gary remained. The agent took up station on Mariana's other side, a silent assurance that they would no longer be alone. Not ever.

They made room for Darren on the bench. Barry was seated in a weathered plastic chair borrowed from the local eatery. Darren settled between Neil and Tanaka, easing himself down in careful stages. He was still extremely fragile from his recent seizure and the accident that preceded it. He wondered about the toll on his body from all this. Not to mention the transits.

Then he decided it didn't really matter.

Tanaka was the same as always, a leather-wrapped stone in a sleeveless sweatshirt and board shorts. Darren asked him, 'How old are you?'

The question reshaped Tanaka's stern features into a rare smile. 'Same as you, bro.'

'Right now I feel a hundred and thirty.'

'Zooming around the stars will do that to you,' Barry offered.

Orna stood next to her husband, one hand resting on Tanaka's shoulder. 'You will heal. Time will work its magic.' She pointed out to sea. 'Especially if you return to the wellspring of your youth.'

Darren shook his head. 'There's no way you'll get me out in that.'

'That' was the calling card of Tropical Storm Carmen, expected to grow into a Category Two hurricane before making landfall somewhere north of Jacksonville. Possibly even a Cat Three. At this point in time, the storm was still a hundred or so miles offshore. The waves carried a thunderous force, and were breaking far out, Darren estimated a quarter mile. Between the peaks and the shore was a solid blanket of foam, backwash, secondary breaks and struggling surfers.

Darren turned to the man seated on his left. Neil had still not glanced his way, nor acknowledged his presence. Darren asked, 'How big do you make them?'

Neil pretended to give it careful consideration. 'Twelve foot, easy.'

'What, twelve?' Barry pointed with the hand not resting on Mariana's chair-back. 'The inside sets are over ten.'

Tanaka laughed. 'That's your fear talking.'

Barry leaned over so as to see around Orna. 'I don't see you out there going for no barrels.'

Tanaka opened his mouth to respond, but Orna was swifter. 'The storm will pass and the sea will calm. When it is time, you will rejoin with the energies of your youth. You will heal. You will prepare. When the season arrives, you will move on to greater things.'

Barry studied her a long moment. 'Why do I feel like you should be on a stage spouting poetry to thousands?'

'Welcome to my world,' Tanaka said.

'Because I speak the truth,' Orna replied. 'And because you are willing to hear it.'

Barry went back to watching the waves. 'Man, it's been so long.'

'Years,' Tanaka agreed.

'Longer,' Darren said. 'Decades.'

Neil remained silent.

Barry said, 'Of course, now that the sale of my hotels and restaurants and some other stuff has gone through, I do have some free time.'

This resulted in some cheers, a couple of high-fives. Which meant they almost missed hearing Mariana say quietly, 'I've always wanted to learn how to surf.'

'And I will teach you,' Orna said. 'Soon as you have the doctor's OK.'

Barry asked, 'You surf?'

'It's been years,' Orna replied. 'Decades. But that's no excuse. Is it, my husband.'

Darren decided the time had come. He turned to Neil and asked, 'What do you say, are you in?'

When Neil faced him, he wore the same expression Darren had seen in the hospital. 'I owe you another apology.'

Darren took his time. Wanting to get it right this time around. 'Did it ever occur to you that you saved my life?'

Neil remained silent. Watchful.

'I'm here because you insisted on coming into my room alone. So you could apologize. Which you didn't need to do, but we're not going there.' Darren held his hand directly in front of Neil's face, silencing the objection, then continued, 'Every minute you made them wait outside my room increased those ladies' anxiety level.'

Barry was the one who said, 'I don't follow.'

'Think about it,' Darren said, his gaze level on Neil. 'They couldn't afford to have me tell somebody I had just missed out on being the third component of an alien invasion. So what happened? The instant you left, they barreled inside with one thing on their minds. Make sure I was permanently silenced. Who knows what might have happened if they thought they had all the time in the world? Discover Evelyn was lurking inside the bathroom? Realize Gary was just pretending to relax out in the corridor? Comprehend both of them were on high alert?'

Tanaka asked, 'They already knew you weren't . . .'

Gary stepped closer to the group. 'We're using the term, infected.'

'Since the moment I opened my eyes in the ambulance,' Darren replied, 'those two knew. I'm certain of it. They traveled in the ambulance because they weren't sure. But long before we arrived at the hospital, they were looking for their chance to take me out.'

Gary offered, 'Evelyn was already worried by their change in behavior. She added that to how Darren was shifting from the dreamstates.' He shrugged. 'The lady is a master at fitting the impossible together and identifying the unseen.'

'Evelyn had to know if I was like Leila and Anchali,' Darren continued. 'Your saying what you did, forcing me to interrupt and beg for help, it clarified my own status.'

Gary added, 'Then the infected pair declared you were their enemy, and Evelyn had all the confirmation we'd ever need.'

Mariana asked, 'You recorded the exchange?'

'Every word,' Gary confirmed.

'I'd like to hear it.'

'Whenever you're ready.'

Her voice was fragile, but steady. 'Am I still on the case?'

Gary actually smiled. 'Colonel, you've been top of the duty roster since day one. Nothing's changed.'

'Good,' Mariana said. 'I'm glad.'

Darren asked Neil, 'So, we're good?'

'Better than that.'

'They want me to stay on the job. Is that what you want too?'

Neil shifted his gaze back to the sea, his face relaxed now, eyes alight. 'I wouldn't have it any other way.'